RAPTOR:

RETRIBUTION OF THE REVENANTS

Matthew Dennion

Cover Art:
Elden Ardiente of Lungga Creatives

Wild Hunt Press

i

This book is dedicated to My Beloved Family.

-- Matt Dennion

Table of Contents

CHAPTER 1 1

CHAPTER 2 8

CHAPTER 3 20

CHAPTER 4 26

CHAPTER 5 35

CHAPTER 6 41

CHAPTER 7 46

CHAPTER 8 56

CHAPTER 9 60

CHAPTER 10 69

CHAPTER 11 76

CHAPTER 12 87

CHAPTER 13 93

CHAPTER 14 101

CHAPTER 15 107

CHAPTER 16 118

CHAPTER 17 126

EPILOGUE 136

ABOUT THE AUTHOR 138

RAPTOR:

RETRIBUTION OF THE REVENANTS

CHAPTER 1

Charles Donner awoke to find that he was in complete darkness. His head was aching, and his body was being bounced around on some hard surface. He was confused as to where he was and what was happening to him. Charles tried to reach up and rub his head. It was at that point, he realized that he could not move his hands. Charles shifted his hands back and forth and he found that they were tied together. He began to panic and attempted to scream but when he did so the sack that was covering his face sank into his mouth.

Charles gagged on the thick potato sack which enveloped his head. He began using his tongue to push the sack out of his mouth. After several failed attempts, Charles managed to work the sack out of his mouth so that he could breathe. After taking a few breaths, he thought about trying to scream once more but thought better of it as he knew he would only end up choking on the potato sack again. His head slammed into something hard above him, exacerbating the pain his skull was already experiencing. After letting out a quiet curse, Charles tried to calm down and remember what had happened to him.

The last thing he could recall doing was watching the baseball game at JD's Bar and Grill. Charles remembered entering the bar with a pocket full of cash. He was eager to spend his money on beer, beef, and broads. He had won big on his last game and he was looking to celebrate before the season ended and he was forced to go out into the real world. Charles groaned as he realized that his performance in his latest game may have been the cause of his current situation. Hence, he thought back on the events of the past several months.

At a well-built '6'5", Charles was the star of Port City University's basketball team. Playing college basketball was not nearly as fun or as rewarding as Charles had thought it would be. He had a full scholarship, but his sports schedule left him little time to study and as result his grades were suffering. He was a good enough college player, but he knew that he was an undersized power forward by NBA standards. It was extremely unlikely that he would find a career playing professional basketball in the States.

There was the chance of playing overseas but that was akin to the minor leagues. He could make a living playing ball in Italy, Turkey, or China but did he really want to? Charles knew he would never be rich from playing basketball in any of those countries and with his grades slipping because of his basketball schedule, he was unlikely to graduate with any kind of useful degree.

That is when an offer came his way that he could not refuse. A man in a business suit calling himself the Barracuda met him outside of his dorm one night. The Barracuda asked Charles to come with him for a couple of drinks. Never being one to turn down free drinks Charles went with the man. Despite his ominous name, the man calling himself the Barracuda was a small, weaselly-looking person. Charles had no doubt that he could easily overpower him if he had too.

They walked to a nearby bar and after ordering drinks the Barracuda leaned in close to Charles and presented an offer he could not refuse. The Barracuda explained that he was well connected in the gambling community and that together the two of them could make a lot of money.

Charles' immediate response was that he would never throw a game. He and his teammates all worked hard to be the best basketball players they could be, and throwing a game was completely out of the question. He would never do that to his friends and cost them wins.

The Barracuda shook his head and smiled. "Who's talking about throwing games? I would never ask you to throw a game. I was thinking more along the lines of just not winning as big as you can each and every time." The Barracuda leaned back in his chair. "You know how point spreads work, right? A bunch of guys in Vegas look at a game and decide that your team should be able to beat another team by a certain amount of points. Then people bet as to whether you beat the other team by that much or not?"

The Barracuda stopped talking as the waitress walked over and gave them their drinks. Charles picked up his beer, chugged down a mouthful of it, looked the Barracuda in the eyes, and said, "You're talking about point shaving."

The Barracuda nodded. "You never have to lose to a game or even come close to losing it. When the game is well in hand, make an errant turnover, don't guard your man so closely, brick a shot or two. When the clock hits zero we both get paid big money."

Charles took a deep breath as the Barracuda continued his pitch. "Look, we both know you're not going pro, right? How much time and effort have you put into college basketball? Shouldn't you make some kind of money out of it?"

Charles looked the Barracuda straight in the eye and uttered, "I will never intentionally throw a game."

The Barracuda grinned. "Like I said, I would never ask you to do that. Just cut a big lead off a game here and there. It will only be every once in a while. If you shave points to many games people will start to notice and it will throw off the point spreads that Vegas gives out. If that starts happening it will make it harder for us to pull this off."

Charles remembered considering the offer one last time. He was an athlete, a competitor, and he wondered if point shaving would weigh on his mind. He then balanced any guilt he was feeling against the work he had put into basketball and the lack of work that commitment was causing him to put into his studies. Charles knew he needed something of monetary value from his college experience and this looked to be his best option.

He reached over and shook the Barracuda's hand. "How does this work?"

The Barracuda smiled, revealing teeth that had been filed down into razors. "It's easy… on the day we are going to go forward with our plan, a representative of mine will slip a piece of paper under your door with a number on it. You make sure that team doesn't win by more than that number. As long as you keep the final score differential under that number, we, and a lot of other people, get paid. Like I said, easy."

After that meeting, Charles would receive a numbered paper roughly every third game or so that he played. He never had to throw a game and the money he was pulling in each game was in the hundreds of thousands. Charles was smart with his money. He kept some of it for pocket money but not enough for anyone in the athletic department to notice that he was spending beyond his means. He put the rest of his cash in a savings account.

It was in his last game that he decided to switch things up. On the morning of his last game, he found a note under his door with the number "16" on it. Charles knew the team he was playing was not nearly as good as his team. He knew that his team could easily beat the point spread. Charles decided that now was the time to act, and to secure his future, while he was in direct control of it. He took all the money that he had been saving up and bet it on his team to cover the point spread. Then the young athlete played the game of his life. He led his team to a blowout victory beating his hapless opponents by more than thirty points. With the bets he had made on his team, Charles had more than tripled his already sizable account.

When the game was over, he let out a sigh of relief. His college career was all but over. All that he had to do now was to sit on his money until he left school and then he could start spending the winnings he had accrued.

If he was asked by the Barracuda about why he didn't comply with the point shaving, he would say that his coach had gotten wise to the scheme. That his coach warned him he had better play up to his potential or he would report him to the NCAA. The NCAA had very harsh penalties for anyone involved in point shaving. They would prosecute him and anyone else connected to the scandal. So, when faced with this choice he thought better of shaving points in that game to protect not only himself but the Barracuda as well.

This brought Charles back to celebration at the bar. He had one too many drinks and then stumbled out the door as the establishment closed. He knew he took at least a few steps toward the parking lot. The next thing that he could remember was finding himself tied up in a small space, with a sack over his head. He began to shake as he realized what had most likely happened to him. The Barracuda must have been angry with him blowing the point spread and sent some of his lackeys to grab him. The hard, shaky surface he was in was probably the trunk of a car, and he was likely being taken to see the Barracuda.

Charles' body was suddenly tossed forward and slammed into the floor of the trunk. A wave of nausea and vertigo swept over him as he heard voices from outside of the car. Then he heard a loud click and a wave of light filled what little vision he had through the sack which was tied around his head. He felt two strong pull him out of the car. He was thrown to the ground hard, cutting his shoulder open as it slammed into the concrete. The scent of salt water crept past the blood that had pooled in his nostrils and he realized that he must be at the Port City docks.

4

Charles heard the Barracuda's voice say, "Cut out eye slits for him. I want him to see what's going to happen to him."

The powerful hand that pulled him out of the car grabbed the back of his head and pulled it forward. A thin knife pierced the sack around his head and scratched the skin under his right eye. Charles yelled in pain as the knife cut through the sack around his left eye and dug into the skin beneath his eyebrow.

Blood flowed over his left eye as he looked up through the newly made slits, to see the razor toothed smile of the Barracuda standing in front of him. The mobster shook his head. "We had a good thing going, Charles, and you had to go and get greedy. I was paying you well, but you decided to screw me over and bet on yourself to beat the spread." He shrugged. "A word of advice: if you are going to screw someone over like that, get your money and get out of town fast. When you stay and flaunt it, you draw attention to yourself. The kind of attention that helps the people you screwed over to find you."

The blood that was flowing into Charles' eye was now mixed with tears as his body shook with fear. "Barracuda, this isn't what it looks like," he pleaded. "I had no choice but to beat the spread. The coach found out about what I was doing. He said if I shaved points off another game that he would report me to the NCAA. Not only would I have gone to jail, but your entire organization would have been in trouble."

The Barracuda laughed and as he did so, Charles could have sworn that he saw what looked like a beautiful blonde woman in tight fitting, short leather clothes, with an open trench coat draped around her shoulders and what looked like a sword attached to her hip standing behind him. Aside from the fact that she was stunningly attractive, there was something about the woman that made Charles yearn for her. It was not a sexual attraction he was feeling. When he looked at the woman, Charles felt as if there was a piece of himself missing and only this woman could fill that void. The basketball player blinked once and the strange woman was gone.

The gangster took a step forward and put his face in front of Charles' eyes. "The coach was going to turn you in? Really? Is that the story you're going with?"

Charles cried as he muttered, "It's the truth. Coach Flanagan found out what I was doing. He confronted me about it this morning in practice. I knew you would be mad if he turned us in. So, I made sure to play as hard as I could. You know, to protect you."

5

The Barracuda nodded. "And part of your idea to protect me involved taking a large sum of money and betting it on yourself to beat the point spread?"

Charles did not know what to say. He was trying to think of a reply that would save his life when the Barracuda slapped him across the face.

The bookies' voice changed from being somewhat friendly to showing how angry he really was. "Let me ask you two questions! First, how stupid do you think I am? Here's a hint: that was a rhetorical question. Don't bother trying to think up a lie about how betting on yourself protects me! Second, do you really think you're the only person on your team that I have on my payroll?"

Charles shrugged, as the realization that a second person being on the Barracuda's payroll was a death sentence for him.

The Barracuda punched Charles in the gut. "That question *wasn't* rhetorical!" he shouted. "But since you clearly don't know the answer let me see if someone else in the class can help you out with it." The mobster looked behind him and said, "Coach, can you tell this schmuck how many people on your teamwork for me?"

Charles saw his coach step into view. He could barely make out the man who had coached him every day for the last four years through the blood and tears that filled his vision. When the man spoke, however, Charles immediately recognized the voice of Ken Flanagan, his coach.

Flanagan shook his head, "We had a good thing going, kid. Going off on your own like that… not a good idea." He shrugged. "You put me in a spot where I couldn't even pull you from the game without the NCAA taking notice and accusing me of point shaving."

Charles wept, "Coach, they're going to kill me."

Flanagan shrugged again and replied, "I wish there was something I could do, kid. The truth is you brought this on yourself. I have my own family to think about, and the fact that you tried to pin this whole thing on me?" Flanagan shook his head. "Well, doing that was low. Any thoughts I had about trying to save you went out the window when you said I was the one who was going to turn you and the Barracuda in."

The Barracuda gestured to whoever was standing behind Charles. "Moose, take this guy out on the boat, weigh him down, run him through, and then toss him over the side. We need to make an example out of him, so people know what happens when they screw us over."

Charles turned around to see a massive man, even larger and thicker than he was, reaching out for him. Charles started screaming for help, but his cry was cut short when Moose kicked him in the stomach and knocked the wind out of him. The young athlete was gasping for breath as he fell to the ground.

Charles tried to sit up as Moose's hands reached down, grabbed him, and then started dragging him toward a small boat. As the young athlete was dragged onto the boat, he saw the woman in the trench coat sitting on the deck. He looked at her, his eyes pleading to her for help, but her only response was to hold her finger to her mouth signaling him to remain silent.

Charles felt thick chains wrap around his arms and legs. He looked up to see Moose above him, and the huge burly man struck him in the stomach again. This once more forced the air out of his lungs and caused him to fall down onto the deck of the boat.

Charles was still gasping for air as the boat started making its way to the middle of the harbor. As the vessel drove out, Charles looked through the eye slits of the sack over his head to see the beautiful but strange woman standing over him. He did his best to mouth the words "Help me."

The woman shrugged and in a hollow voice replied, "Not yet." She then stepped back as Moose came over and lifted Charles to the side of the ship.

Charles was looking down at the water when he felt a sharp pain first in his back and then in his chest. He looked down to see the blade of a machete sticking out of his torso. His head shifted to the side so that only one of his eyes was still lined up with an eye slit and he saw Moose reaching for him. The mob enforcer pulled the knife out of the basketball player, then lifted him over the side of the boat, and tossed him into the estuary.

Charles felt his mouth and lungs filling with both blood and water as the cold water of the harbor made his body go numb. When the weight of the chains brought him to the bottom of the dock, he saw the woman in the tight-fitting clothes and the trench coat with the sword standing in front of him. With his last breath, Charles mouthed the words, "Help me."

The woman smiled at him and said, "In just a few more moments, I will give you all the help you could ever require."

Charles looked at her in desperation, and her angelic face was the last thing he saw before he died.

CHAPTER 2

Ben Watkins was staring out the window at the sun as it slowly dipped behind the building on the Western side of Port City. From his office, he could see the entire skyline of the city. To his right, he could see the watchtower atop city hall and the water tower atop the Grinnon Building. As he turned his head to his left, he saw the courthouse directly across the street from his building and farther down the street the city jail. Atop the courthouse he could see the statue of Justice, holding her scales above the city. Watkins had always appreciated that the people who built the statue made actual functional scales for the sculpture as opposed to one of immobile stone.

On any given day, Watkins could look out his window and see the scales balancing themselves. The jail, of course, had the guard tower standing over the yard, like a giant sentinel warning anyone who committed a crime of what their fate would be.

He checked his watch as Chester Mansfield continued to drone on with his newest proposed investment for his company.

Watkins continued to stare out the window until Mansfield raised his voice and said, "Mr. Watkins, are you even listening to me? I know how you feel about Watkins Technologies accepting contracts from the military but the potential profits to the company would be huge. We could more than double the price of our stock."

Ben's face lit up with anger at Mansfield's words. The well-built, '6'2", 220-pound Watkins crossed the long boardroom in four quick steps. He pressed his chest up against Mansfield and then looked down at the small man.

"You know how I feel about military contracts." He shook his head. "You may know my history with military contracts and with military grade weapons, but I assure you that you do not know my feelings. My family -- my entire family, my parents and siblings -- were all killed by terrorists. Terrorists who at the time they carried out this act were part of an actual military."

Watkins glared down at Mansfield before continuing his spiel. "Since I founded this company, Watkins Technologies has made its fortune by developing weapons and armaments for law enforcement. For the people who get up every day and try to save lives, not for those who look to go abroad killing others. Additionally, this company's profits have gone up every year for the past five years. This company is now worth several billion dollars"

Mansfield took a step back from the much larger Ben Watkins and replied, "Yes, Mr. Watkins, I understand that, but the current offer from the military will make us more money than we have made in the past three years combined."

Watkins put his hands in the air in front of him with his palms out, signaling Mansfield to stop talking. "The current contract offer from the military will assure that our technology is used to kill people on the battlefield in some far away land. By simply maintaining our current contracts we will continue to grow and profit while assuring that our technology stays here in the U.S. and works to save the lives of our citizens."

Mansfield was about to say something else when Watkins cut him off with, "If you don't care for that option, then may I remind you that I still own 65% of Watkins Technologies. I am also the CEO and chief scientist for this company. It's my inventions and patents that keep this company in the black, and it's my decisions that run it. This board functions in an advisory capacity. I have listened to your advice on this topic in the past and turned it down. I am doing so again today. I suggest that if you would like to keep your job, you will honor my wishes as to how we deploy our technology!"

Mansfield was shaking from mixed emotions of anger and fear. He swallowed hard and looked at his superior. "I will follow your wishes and table the idea of selling our products to military establishments."

Ben nodded and said, "Thank you, Mr. Mansfield." He then turned to look at the rest of the board. "Is there anything else that we need to address before we start off our weekends?"

A woman spoke up from the back of the conference table. "Mr. Watkins, the American History Museum will be hosting the Ulysses S. Grant attraction for the next several weeks. This exhibit has been completely funded by donations from the Watkins Foundation. The museum curator was hoping that you could be there for the display's opening this Monday."

Watkins replied, "I strongly believe in helping to encourage education and cultural awareness in the city. I will be more than happy to appear at the museum on Monday morning. I'll have my assistant confirm that I'll be there and ask her to add it to my schedule."

Watkins looked over his board to see if there were any other topics to be addressed. When nobody else spoke up Watkins smiled, "Ladies and gentlemen," he announced, "it's getting late, it's Friday, and I don't want to keep you from your families. Thank you for all that you do and please have a wonderful weekend and be safe. We all know how dangerous it can be in Port City."

The members of the board all stood up, bid Ben farewell, and then shuffled out of the office. Mansfield was the only one who said nothing to his employer. The money hungry little man simply sighed and left the board room. Mansfield went to the restroom, entered a stall, and closed the door.

When he was sure no one else was around he took out his phone and sent a text. *Watkins would not accept the contract offer. No need to worry yet, I am confident that I can convince him to accept it when presented with additional data.* Mansfield watched his phone nervously as the person he had texted was formulating a reply.

When the reply came up it read, *You, had better be able to convince him to accept the contract. You have no idea how many volatile pieces are connected to this puzzle.*

Mansfield's body shook as he placed the phone back into his pocket and exited the restroom.

***

Once the boardroom had emptied out, Ben Watkins took an elevator that led to his private laboratory beneath the Watkins Building. He quickly checked a few new projects he had been working on. These mainly consisted of prototypes in various stages of development that Watkins' company sold to law enforcement organizations. He made a few quick adjustments to a long range taser he had been working on and he recently had some new ideas for. After working on the taser, he moved to the wall in the back of the lab.

Watkins reached out and touched a seemingly innocuous panel on the wall. When he touched the panel, it caused the wall to slide open and reveal a hidden corridor. As Ben walked into the passage, the section of the wall closed behind him. He found himself in an abandoned section of an old subway tunnel. Ben sprinted down the old tracks for roughly half a mile until he came to a transport that was resting on the tracks.

The transport looked like a single rail car to a subway train with the exception that its front end had a beak-like shape to it and the outside of the transport was painted brown with white dots, giving it a color pattern similar to that of a hawk or an owl.

Watkins jumped into the transport and closed the door. He then gave a verbal command, "Take me to the lair." The command had no sooner left his mouth than the transport sped down the old tracks.

As the transport was moving, Ben pressed a button that caused a compartment to extend from the interior wall of the vehicle. He looked down to see an exo-suit, gauntlets, a beak-shaped helmet with a visor, two bandoliers filled with spheres, and a cape inside of it. Ben changed out of his business clothing and into the exo-suit. The bulletproof exo-suit mirrored the color design of the transport. As Watkins pulled the suit over his toned body, he felt it lock into place over his muscles. The exo-suit increased Ben Watkins' already considerable strength by at least three-fold. Watkins flexed his arms, and as he did so he felt as if he had the power to lift a horse over his head if he needed to.

Next Watkins took out the sphere-filled bandoliers and strapped them around his chest. As he did so, he took inventory of each of the spheres attached to his chest. The devices were special non-lethal weapons that Watkins had created. Each sphere had a different function, including explosives, electrical charge, gas dispersal, fire retardant, liquid nitrogen dispersal, and some were simply solid spheres to be used as throwing weapons.

Once the bandoliers were in place, Ben grabbed the cape and attached it to the exo-suit at the shoulders. Like the exo-suit, the cape was bulletproof and colored brown with white stripes. In addition to being bulletproof, the cape also had the capability of working as a semi-parachute to slow a fall from a high altitude.

11

After fitting the cape into place, Ben put on the gauntlets. Each of the gauntlets was the same light brown as the suit. The wrists were wreathed by a series of thick muzzles. Inside the muzzles, were additional non-lethal baton-like projectiles that had a range far greater than he could ever throw a sphere even with his enhanced strength. Like the spheres, each of the batons had a different purpose.

Ben Watkins took a deep breath, before reaching down and picking up the thick helmet with the beak-shaped visor. He took a moment to look at his reflection in the screen before pulling it over his head. Of all Raptor's crime fighting equipment, the helmet and visor were his greatest tools. As Ben Watkins, he had developed the world's most advanced supercomputer complete with a fully functional AI system. That system was linked to the visor in his helmet. With only a verbal command, Raptor could find any information he wanted on the Web, override virtually any computerized system, and control his entire arsenal remotely. Raptor's mastery of technology made him one of the most dangerous men on the planet.

Once the helmet connected to the exo-suit, a digital array showing all manner of information appeared in Ben's field of view. As he looked at the information streaming before him, he had completed the transition from Ben Watkins, inventor and businessman, to the vigilante known as Raptor.

Raptor cracked his neck as he gave the command which initiated the AI that was operating in his visor, "Activate Eagle Eye protocol."

Instantly, Raptor was given back door access to all media and law enforcement databases and servers. As one of the world's top computer programmers his company had won contracts to install the infrastructure for Port City's police department, FBI offices, DHS, and even what Raptor knew was a small company that operated as a CIA front.

Raptor's keen mind sifted through the data stream and singled out key points of information he was looking for. There were numerous crimes that potentially warranted his attention, but his eyes stopped when he saw a police report on the disappearance of Torrol Johnson. The latter was an informant that Raptor had utilized on multiple occasions. He was also a former pimp and drug dealer.

After serving his time in jail, he immediately tried to pick up where his old life had left off. Raptor followed the former inmate and as he was trying to make his first drug sale, the hero swung down from a nearby building and scared off the potential buyer. At the sight of Raptor, Johnson fell to his knees and begged the vigilante for mercy. Knowing that fighting crime extended beyond simply thrashing criminals and putting them behind bars, Raptor made an offer to the ex-con.

The former felon had connections that Raptor could never attain. He could infiltrate the criminal underworld and feed the masked crusader information on the activities of numerous gangs and criminals. Raptor offered Johnson a chance to atone for his crimes by operating as an informant.

In order to compensate the new informant for his services, Raptor would provide the informant with weekly payments that would allow him to live a comfortable but not luxurious lifestyle. The former criminal's options were to accept the offer and agree not to engage in any more criminal activity, or to return to prison. Johnson accepted the offer and had been working for Raptor ever since.

His latest tip had put Raptor on to the trail of an illegal dog fighting ring that had cropped up in the city.

The report indicated that Johnson was last seen outside Madison Nightclub. His friends said they had walked out of the club with him and were making their way to the subway when a large cargo van pulled alongside them. Several men in ski masks jumped out of the rear of the van, pointed guns at Johnson and his friends, and ordered the former's friends to back away. They then grabbed the informant and threw him in the back of the cargo van.

The kidnapping had taken place on the previous night and the police had still not made any progress on the case. Raptor surmised that the disappearance of a known felon like Torrol was low on their priority list. He, however, considered the man to be of the utmost importance. Not only did Johnson provide him with vital information, but he also had a personal connection to Raptor. Johnson was an example of Raptor turning a criminal's life around. To Raptor, Johnson was proof that he could do more than just bring justice to the guilty; he was proof that he could turn a man's life around, and truly make the world a better place.

Raptor quickly recalled the list of potential locations that Johnson had given him where tonight's dog fights would occur. Raptor had learned long ago that when an abduction took place it usually occurred not far from where the kidnappers intended to take their victim. In this instance, there were two places where dog fights were occurring tonight that were within a 20-block radius of where Johnson was taken.

As the transport came to a stop, Raptor considered the two options and decided to start with the location closest to the nightclub. The hero stepped out of the transport and into the underground facility that served as his base of operations. As Ben Watkins, Raptor had purchased several abandoned warehouses along the river. For a man of Watkins' means, procuring something like the warehouse was an everyday occurrence. He purposely kept the buildings nearly empty. Aside from a few computers, printers, and tables to work on there was nothing in the warehouse.

If anyone asked why he had made this purchase, his response was very practical: he used them for a tax write off. Once the warehouses were his, Watkins hired several different companies in shifts to dig out the ground underneath the buildings and deliver or install different types of equipment. Slowly over the years, piece by piece, Ben Watkins would assemble the base he would operate from as Raptor.

The base itself was entirely pitch black. Aside from helping to keep anyone who managed to get inside the warehouses above it from deciding to look at the building's lower levels and what was beneath them; the lack of lights also made Ben Watkins wear his visor while he was inside his lair.

Raptor's visor had the most up to date night vision technology embedded in it. Through the lenses of this device, the completely black base looked as if it was an outside establishment at noon on a sunny day. Having to wear his visor inside the lair forced him to be in his Raptor persona as opposed to his civilian identity. Ben Watkins would never be able to operate effectively in his base. Hence, when he was in his lair, he was always Raptor.

The center of the hero's den was split into two halves. The front half was a gym that was comparable to the best exercise facilities in the city. The training center had free weights and machine weights, a speed bag and heavy bag for boxing training. The lair also had numerous cardio machines including an elliptical machine, a stationary bike, a rowing machine, and a treadmill. All these amenities surrounded a series of mats where Raptor practiced the numerous martial arts and fighting techniques that he had mastered over the years.

The back half of the lair's center had been transformed into a crime lab that rivaled the FBI at their headquarters in Washington, DC. The lab was sectioned off into specialized areas for analysis including biological, chemical, toxicological, fingerprinting, and a firearms section. The latter section looked like a second fully stocked arsenal as Raptor had a variety of weapons from handguns and hunting rifles to military grade armaments. The vigilante used these weapons to conduct various tests on the evidence he found at crime scenes.

The final aspect of Raptor's underground crime lab was a trace evidence section. This area was equipped with a variety of microscopes including a traditional microscope, an electron microscope, an FTIR microscope, and comparison microscopes.

Against the back wall of Raptor's base of operations was a massive computer array with at least six different screens. This was the array which was linked to his visor. This system gave Raptor instant access to any information he may need, and also allowed him to always be at the helm of his automated crime fighting arsenal.

The right wall was covered with the spheres and batons that Raptor used as part of his crime fighting arsenal. If the hero returned from a mission and needed to restock his weapons this is where he would gather them from.

As he was looking at the wall, the transport that brought him to his base rolled to stop on a set of tracks that ran parallel to this partition. Raptor watched for a moment as a mechanical arm reached out from the transport and began selecting weapons from the shelf. The Artificial Intelligence that Raptor had installed in the transport was ensuring that the next time Ben Watkins made the journey from his office to his lair to transform into Raptor, his exo-suit arsenal would be fully stocked.

Lined up along the left wall were nearly another dozen exo-suits. Roughly half of the suits were just like the one Raptor currently wore. The remaining suits were created for more specific tasks such as operating underwater or at high altitudes. Next to the suits were a series of motorcycles. Like his uniforms, the vigilante's motorcycles were specially equipped for crime fighting purposes.

Behind the motorcycles was a long tunnel that led into the city's large storm drain system and emptied out by the river. Finally, next to the bikes were two aerial drones that the vigilante had patched into his visor so that he could control it while still operating independently from it. The drones had been developed by Raptor and his personal pilot Isabell Mendez. Isabell was one of only two people who knew that Ben Watkins was Raptor. Her experience in the Air Force was crucial in helping the costumed vigilante to adapt the drones for use in a city.

The hero had a determined look on his face as he turned and climbed onto his motorcycle. He hoped that he had made the correct decision as to which dog fighting site to investigate first as he sped off down the corridor that led to the river.

As he was speeding down the tunnel, the hero spoke into his visor, "Activate drone."

The command caused a five foot by five-foot stealth drone to spring to life in Raptor's lair. The machine rose into the air and then followed Raptor down the storm drain. When the vigilante's cycle exited a large storm drain that ended near the river, the hero veered to the side and drove out of the drain system and onto the street. Simultaneously, the drone flew directly above Raptor and matched the speed of his motorcycle.

The drone provided the hero with an aerial view of the city around him as well as enough firepower to destroy a house if needed. Raptor clenched his teeth and floored his cycle as he headed for the first destination on his list in the hope that he was not too late to save Torrol Johnson.

The vigilante weaved in and out of traffic as he made his way toward the former Fish Bucket warehouse along the river. The building was only a few miles from where Raptor had exited the storm drain, but the quickest way to reach the warehouse called for him to use some of the city's main streets. As he passed cars his helmet showed him the social media feed of people in their cars posting that Raptor had just driven past them.

The hero spoke into his visor, "Initiate media disruption protocols."

As the words left Raptor's mouth, the mini-supercomputer in his visor sent out an algorithm he had written which changed the information being shared over the Net about him. Street names, times, and even the dates of posts were instantly changed. The hero wanted Port City to know he was out there. He wanted the criminals to know he was chasing them down and at the same time, he hoped that his presence gave the people of Port City some kind of hope. What he didn't want were large groups of civilians trying to follow him as he headed into dangerous territory. With his algorithm distorting his movements on social media, Raptor turned off the heavily traveled street and cut through several alleyways, before turning onto a relatively abandoned street heading toward the warehouse.

The hero pulled his cycle to a stop outside of the warehouse and then had his drone fly around the building to perform a thermal imaging scan. The scan revealed that there were at least fifty people in the building and numerous dogs. Raptor now knew that the ring of criminals he was looking for was operating in this location. He just hoped that Johnson was inside the building.

The thermal scan had shown that four guards were at the front door and nearly a dozen more were stationed by the loading docks at the back of the building. Everyone else in the edifice were gathered around the dog ring in the center of the first floor. The bay doors were made of steel and only a few inches thick. A review of the building's blueprints showed that the doors were not weight bearing. The vigilante decided that an attack on the bay doors was the best option to draw attention from the main entrance to gain access to the building.

Raptor positioned his drone near the bay doors at the back of the building. The device hovered for a few seconds as he determined the appropriate amount of firepower to blow through the barrier while simultaneously minimizing the risk of casualties to the guards. Raptor had no qualms about injuring criminals, but he despised killing people and avoided doing so at all costs.

With the proper amount of firepower determined, Raptor had the drone fire two low yield missiles. The missiles exploded against the doors, sending shrapnel flying through the interior of the building. Most of the guards in the back were knocked unconscious from the blast. The three guards who were still conscious were too disoriented or injured to present a threat. The hero kept the drone in a hovering position at the opening to block any of the people in the building from leaving.

The guards at the front door were all focused on the explosion at the back of the building, allowing Raptor to enter through the front door. The vigilante struck one of the guards in the back of the head knocking him unconscious. The guard standing next to the man who Raptor had just knocked out turned around to see the hero's fist coming toward his face. The vigilante hit the guard with enough force to shatter the man's nose and incapacitate him. Seeing their fellow guards knocked down, the remaining two sentries rushed to attack Raptor.

The guard to Raptor's left pointed his gun at the hero. The crime fighter used a quick snap kick to send the gun flying out of the man's hand. The move was followed by a stiff jab that knocked the guard off balance. The last guard was sprinting toward Raptor when the vigilante dropped to the ground and used his leg to sweep the man at his knees. The fourth sentry fell to the ground bouncing his head off the concrete floor. As the guard was trying to pull himself off the ground, Raptor delivered a hammer fist to the man's temple, knocking him out.

The hero then flipped up from the floor and grabbed the man whose gun he had kicked away. He pulled the guard so close to him that the man's nose was pressed against his visor. Raptor growled at the man, "Where's the guy running the show here?"

The guard pointed to the ring in the center of the building. Raptor drove his helmet into the man's skull knocking him out. He then looked to the dog pit to see a man in a tuxedo coughing and trying to clear the smoke and dust from the back of the building away from his eyes and mouth.

Raptor dashed across the floor of the warehouse and grabbed the well-dressed man by his lapels. The hero screamed at the criminal, "Where is Torrol Johnson? What did you do to him?"

The man was shaking with fear as he looked into Raptor's visor. "He's not here," the man stammered. "The boss has him at the main ring over on Polk Street."

In his mind, Raptor cursed at the realization he had chosen the wrong site to attack. He knocked the man out with an uppercut then he yelled out a command into his visor, "Access the police and animal control! Have them send out units to this location as quickly as possible."

Raptor then turned to see the numerous people who had been around the dog pit betting on the deaths of the poor animals as they tried making their way to the blown open bay doors in an attempt to flee the building.

The hero gave out another command into his visor: "Drone, fire a salvo of rubber bullets at the floor in front of the bay doors. Then maintain position until given further orders."

The drone responded to the request, and as the rubber bullets struck the floor it caused the people trying to make their ways to the bay doors to back up into the building.

Raptor turned on a megaphone application in his visor to amplify his voice before saying, *"Stay where you are! The police are on their way! You are going to be arrested for the crime of betting on illegal dog fights! If you attempt to leave, the drone will fire upon you!"*

The gathered dog fighting enthusiasts backed away from the bay doors. Raptor quickly secured the guards and the ringmaster with zip ties. He then ran out the door, leaped onto his cycle, and took off for the other dog fighting ring.

As he was driving away, he yelled into his visor, "Drone, when police cars are within two blocks from current position, break off holding pattern and then fly to my position!"

With the first dog fighting site taken care of, Raptor once more pushed his bike to the limit despite being fully aware that he was too late to save Torrol Johnson.

CHAPTER 3

Torrol Johnson was with a beautiful blonde woman wearing a leather halter top and skirt along with a long black coat at his favorite club.

He did not know the woman's name, he did not remember how he had arrived at the club with her, and he didn't know why she had a sword attached to her waist. None of those details concerned him at that moment, however. The woman was beautiful, and more than that there was something else alluring about her. Something that drew Johnson to her. It was as if she had something that Johnson had never known he needed until now. The ex-convict could not quite understand what was going on, but it was almost as if the woman he was with had cast a spell on him.

They were enjoying a drink when the girl motioned for Johnson to follow her to the dance floor. As he went to make his way to the designated space, he felt as if he was moving through quicksand. It was as if they were stuck on the floor as he tried to move forward. He looked at the blonde and the various people dancing, and to him it seemed as if they were all moving in slow motion. Johnson was staring at the slow-moving people in front of him when he felt a bucket of cold-water splash over his face.

The former criminal shook his head as the clear liquid poured down his upper body. As his vision cleared, he found himself in the middle of a cage with people all around him shouting and cheering. He looked up to see a thin Caucasian man with a shaved head standing above him and holding an empty bucket of water. Johnson recognized the man as Paul Audrey, the head of the dog fighting ring, as well as other illegal endeavors such as prostitution and drug sales. Standing behind Audrey was the woman Johnson had just thought he was on the dance floor with.

Audrey tossed the bucket aside as he bent down and looked at Johnson. "You okay there, Johnson? We knocked you out but then we kept you out with a concoction of several drugs we keep on hand. Sometimes they can cause pretty trippy dreams. I find that a bucket of ice water to the face usually helps to snap people back into awareness."

Johnson heard barking and snarling from outside of the fence. He turned his head to see two huge pit bulls being restrained by their handlers. The mistreated dogs were eager for a chance to enter the ring and tear each other apart. Johnson saw the woman standing behind Audrey move toward him. As she came toward the informant, she still looked as if she were moving in slow motion like she was part of a dream.

Audrey noticed that Johnson was looking past him, and he slapped him in the face, "We keep an eye on all of our people, Johnson. We know that you've been talking to Raptor. Now why would you be talking to that nut in a costume unless you were giving him information on us?"

Johnson shook his head as his body quaked with fear. "No, Paul, I wouldn't rat on you," he muttered. "You know that I'm good. I always do what you ask me to, don't I? You can't say I don't. Raptor was trying to shake me down, but I didn't break. I just gave him some false info, that's all."

Audrey smiled as he replied, "You gave Raptor some bad information and he did nothing to you. He just let you go with giving him bad information? I find that hard to believe." He shrugged. "What really gave you away was the money you've been spending recently. We know you met with Raptor, and we know that you've been spending a lot more money than you usually do."

Audrey punched Johnson in the stomach. The parolee doubled over from the punch and coughed several times, then he looked up to see the leather-clad blonde with the sword sticking out of her belt standing behind Audrey. She was gazing down at him with a look of utter pity.

Audrey picked Johnson up and looked into his eyes. "I'm not surprised you didn't puke from that punch," he said, "considering that you already spilled your guts to Raptor." He then grabbed Johnson's head and turned it toward the dog on the right-hand side of the cage. "Because of you, Raptor has been sticking his beak into my business. That's costing me a lot of money, Johnson.

The good news is you have the chance to make some of that money back for me."

Audrey pushed the young man to the ground. Johnson fell onto his backside with such force that he was pretty sure his tailbone was bruised if not broken from hitting the concrete floor. Johnson looked up to see the blonde standing next to him as Audrey gestured to someone standing outside of the cage. A thick white stick came flying over the fence and Audrey caught it.

Audrey held the stick out to the informant. "Do you know what this is, Johnson? I'll tell you. It's the thigh bone of the last guy who ratted me out. He also cost me money, and like you he had the chance to make me some of that money back. All he had to do to get me my money back was to survive, and that's all you'll have to do as well."

Audrey dropped the leg bone at Johnson's feet before continuing his lecture. "Not live out the rest of your life, of course. You are going to die tonight. The only question is how quickly and how painfully you die."

Audrey gestured to the two raging dogs on either side of the cage. "You're going to use this bone to fight off the dogs for as long as you can, and we're going to bet on how long you make it. If you manage to kill both dogs, then I will put a bullet through your head, and you'll be out of your misery quickly. Of course, if you don't kill the dogs then they will kill you and that will be very unpleasant."

He looked at the leg bone before continuing again. "The guy who that bone belonged to was killed by the dogs. He screamed for so long as the dogs tore him apart. You'd think a pit bull could kill a person pretty quickly, but it took nearly ten minutes for that guy to die." He shrugged. "I'm sure from his perspective, it felt like a lot longer than ten minutes."

Audrey stood up and said "I think you're a fighter though, Johnson. Don't let me down."

Audrey was walking away as the blonde just stood next to the unfortunate former prisoner. He looked at her as she continued to gaze at him with an expression of pity.

"Please help me," he pleaded to her. "You can convince Paul that I didn't rat him out to Raptor. Please don't let the dogs get me."

The woman shrugged and responded in a hollow voice, "I'm sorry. I cannot help you yet. When the time comes, I will allow you to gain retribution on Audrey and all of those placing wagers on your demise."

Audrey slammed the door to the cage shut as a bell sounded and the two dogs were placed in entrances leading to the cage. The blonde backed away from Johnson, but she didn't leave the enclosure.

Johnson leapt in front of her and screamed, "Get behind me!"

The woman calmly replied, "Those beasts cannot hurt me. Besides, I am here as much for them as I am for you."

Johnson turned away from the mysterious woman as the two snarling canines sprinted at him from both sides. He swung the leg bone at the dog charging him from the right. He struck the animal in the head with as much force as he could muster. The blow knocked the dog's head to the side but did nothing to slow the canine's momentum. The dog continued to move forward and crashed into the condemned man's leg, sending the informant falling to the ground. As Johnson hit the concrete, the dog on his right bit down into his forearm and yanked it back and forth in an attempt to rip the limb off his body. The informant was screaming in pain as the canine on his left sank its teeth into his shoulder.

Johnson's blood and pieces of his skin were being thrown into his face as he screamed and tried to free himself from the dogs' grips. The injured man used all of his strength to stand up and in the process, he managed to dislodge the dog that was attacking his shoulder. He then kicked the beast in the ribs that was mauling his right arm and he briefly managed to force the beast off him.

The dog on his left then bit into his leg causing Johnson to focus his attention back toward his left. Johnson looked over to see the blonde woman standing calmly against the bars of the cage watching the event as if the horror occurring to him were an everyday event for her.

The second dog bit into Johnson's other leg and dragged him to the ground. The vicious creatures each tore a mouthful of flesh out of the informant's legs before they tried to mount him. When both dogs were on his chest, they started to fight each other above him. Each of the bloodthirsty creatures was determined to be the one who landed the killing blow. As the canine killers fought their claws raked across Johnson's chest and ripped huge gashes into his torso.

One of the dogs cast off the other and then looked down at Johnson. In a last-ditch attempt to save himself, Johnson tried to strike the dog in the face with the leg bone. The animal caught the bone in its mouth, however. In a fearsome display of how powerful its bite force was the beast crunched the

23

young man's femur in half. The canine then latched its jaws onto Johnson's throat, and he felt the dog's teeth puncture his jugular. This ghastly wound sent blood pouring down his throat and into his lungs. Johnson moaned as he looked over at the blonde woman.

The dog that was killing Johnson was then attacked by the second animal. Johnson held his throat as the two raging beasts mauled each other. After several brutal seconds of battle, one dog managed to kill the other. The victorious but badly wounded dog then turned its attention toward Johnson. It growled and leaped at him. Knowing that he was dying but determined to take the dog with him, the informant grabbed one half of the broken leg bone that was his weapon. When the dog lunged at him, the dying man drove the jagged end of the leg bone into the animal's chest, piercing its heart and lungs. The dog whimpered twice before it died.

Johnson was still holding his neck, choking on his own blood, while a cheer rang out from the frenzied crowd. Audrey walked into the blood-soaked cage and looked down at the dying young man.

"I knew you were a fighter!" the man said with sadistic glee. "You made me some money back and I'm a man of my word."

Audrey took a gun out of his pocket and shot Johnson in the head, ending his life.

As the crowd cheered the blonde walked over to the mutilated Johnson. She bent down and kissed the dead man. Then she ran her hand over the two dead dogs. Audrey was still soaking in the cheers of the crowd as Johnson's and the dogs' bodies stood up and began walking toward each other.

Audrey and the crowd watched in horror as the dead canines walked into Johnson and seemed to be absorbed into his body. The young man's body shifted and moved as the dogs' legs began to protrude out his torso, giving the dead man the look of having eight additional arms sticking out of his ribs. Johnson's shoulders shook as the pit bulls' two heads ripped apart his skin and took positions on either side of his head.

The three-headed and blood-soaked monstrosity turned its trio of heads toward Audrey and roared. The criminal ringmaster turned to run but the blonde woman gestured with her hands towards the gate and it swung closed. Audrey tried to force the gate open, but he was unable to do so. He turned to see the grotesque form of Johnson merged with the two pit bulls moving toward him.

Audrey pulled his gun out and screamed, "Stay the hell away from me!"

The gangster then emptied his clip into the monster. The bullets buried themselves in the ghoul's chest and even into Johnson's forehead, but they did nothing to slow the creature's approach. Audrey was now the one screaming for help as the amalgamated horror reached out with two human arms and grabbed him by the wrists.

The crowd that had been there to watch the dog fights were transfixed by the violent spectacle before them as the eight-dog legs took turns slashing into Paul Audrey's body. After only a few slashes, the criminal's entire chest and stomach were reduced to nothing but blood and long strings of tattered flesh.

Audrey was moaning in pain as he looked up to see the three heads of the creatures, he sentenced to death staring at him. The two dog heads latched onto Audrey's shoulders as Johnson's face stared into Audrey's eyes. The informant's head roared once and then he sank his teeth into Audrey's throat and tore it out.

Blood poured down Johnson's chin as he threw his head back in ecstasy from gaining his revenge. All three heads then turned to look at the blonde.

She smiled as she looked back at the multi-headed revenant. "Who else here?" she queried. "Who else do you blame for your deaths?"

All three heads glared at the gathered crowd that had watched the now merged trio die for their amusement in their respective previous lives.

The blonde nodded. "The crowd who came to cheer and place wages on your deaths and your pain." She nodded again and concurred, "Yes, they too deserve your retribution."

With a wave of her hand the blonde threw open the gate to the cage. The people who had been watching the horrific events in the ring turned and ran for the exits.

With a second wave of her hand, the blonde shut the doors to the warehouse. The first group of people who reached the barred exits tried to pull them open but despite their best efforts, the doors remained shut.

The raving patrons of the dog fights were gathered like livestock at a slaughterhouse as the undead creature made by the blonde femme fatale began tearing into them.

CHAPTER 4

Raptor pulled his cycle to a stop in front of the second warehouse where he knew the dog fighting ring was operating. His drone had just caught up to him and he was about to have it perform a scan of the building when he heard people banging on the exit doors and screams of pain and fear coming from inside the building. The hero expected to hear screaming when he arrived at the scene, but that they would be the wild cheers of a crowd wrapped up in their bloodlust, not those of people in panic.

Raptor ran up to the door where he could hear people trying to force it open and escape whatever was taking place inside of it. The vigilante grabbed the door and pulled on it. Even with his own naturally considerable strength enhanced by his exo-suit the doors did not budge. Raptor let go of the door handles in disbelief as he thought to himself that nothing short of an industrial bank lock should have been able to withstand the pressure he had just exerted on it.

The hero looked at the door itself. It was made of a hardwood and it was several inches thick, but he was sure he could drive his foot through it with a well-placed kick. Raptor lifted his leg and drove it into the door. To his surprise, the vigilante was thrown back as if he had kicked a brick wall.

Raptor shook his head. "Whatever is going on with that door, it's defying the laws of physics." He heard more screams coming from the other side of the entrance and then he looked down to see blood seeping out from the bottom of it.

Knowing that he had only moments left to act if he planned to save anyone inside the warehouse, the hero looked to the nearest window roughly ten feet above him. He grabbed one of the explosive spheres on his bandoliers and threw it at the window. The sphere exploded sending glass raining down at Raptor's feet and on whoever was standing beneath the window inside the warehouse. Raptor knew he might have just injured some of the people in the building but at this point he figured that being injured and alive was better than dead. To make sure that is what happened, he had to get into the warehouse.

The crime fighter used his gauntlet to fire a grappling hook into the window and then pulled back to secure it. He then climbed up to the opening and looked down into the warehouse. As he peered downwards, Raptor gasped at the carnage taking place below him.

On the floor of the warehouse, he could see body parts and blood being tossed into the air as some large creature was tearing into the people trapped there. With more than half of the people in the warehouse already dead, Raptor did not have a second to waste. The vigilante grabbed hold of the chord connected to his grappling hook and then swung down at the monster who was attacking the trapped people.

The hero drove his feet into the monster's blood-soaked chest and knocked the beast back several feet. He then screamed, "Get away from the door!"

The people who had been trying to break down the door backed away from the exit. As they moved from the egress, many of the dog fight patrons slipped and fell on the gore and entrails that littered the floor. Once Raptor had a clear line of sight to the exit, he removed one of the explosive spheres from the bandoliers on his chest and threw it at the door.

The sphere exploded on impact and sent pieces of the destroyed door flying into the parking lot. Raptor was about to yell for the people to run when the beast that he had kicked away a moment ago leaped onto his back. The weight of the creature drove the hero to the ground. He could feel the monstrosity biting at both of his shoulders at the same time. From the pressure he felt, Raptor was certain if it were not for his armor-like exo-suit that both of his shoulders would have been torn off.

The crime fighter tried to push himself up, but the weight of the amalgamated monster was too much for him to overcome. In desperation, Raptor yelled a command into his visor: "Activate exo-suit external shock defense."

The command sent thousands of volts of electricity surging through Raptor's suit. The sudden jolt forced the hybrid monster to release his grip on the vigilante.

The beast rolled away from Raptor, stood up, glared at the armored hero, and then roared at him.

With the horror now standing in front of him, Raptor finally got a good look at the thing he was fighting. The caped hero gasped as he shook his head in disbelief. "Torrol, my God. What have they done to you?"

The beast looked to his left and then turned his head back to Raptor as he responded in a growling voice, "Retribution has given us the means to gain revenge on those that murdered us! Now step aside so that we may have our vengeance!"

When it was done speaking all three heads of the monster looked to its left again. When Raptor noticed this, he quickly shouted a command into his visor: "Shift through all visual outputs!"

Raptor followed the monster's line of sight as his visor showed him an array of views including thermal, ultraviolet, and x-ray. When his visor showed him the electromagnetic activity occurring in the area, he saw the outline of a young woman standing to the left of the creature.

Raptor called out, "Who or what are you, and what's your connection to Torrol?"

The shape of the woman dressed in leather with a sword hanging from her waist looked back at Raptor and replied, "Your visor allows you to see me? That is impressive." She shrugged, "I suppose there is no need to keep myself hidden around you." She waved her hand in front of herself and appeared in the form of the young blonde woman in leather clothing and a long black jacket that Torrol and Charles had seen prior to their deaths. "You will no longer need to see me through your visor. You can see me as those who require my services do."

She then looked toward the monster and said, "Be patient for a moment. We will still gain revenge on those who murdered you."

The strange girl then turned her head back toward Raptor before speaking again. "You may call me Retribution. I have been known by many names over the centuries, Adrestia, Praxidice, Poena. I am the attendant of the aspect of Nemesis for what your mind would comprehend as God. When the Egyptians had their first born slain for keeping the Jews as slaves it was I who did the slaying. When the French nobles had their people turn on them and behead them in the streets it was I who led the peasants. When those in jail who have defiled and murdered children are slain by their fellow inmates it is I who provided them the opportunity. When a horrible crime is committed and the one who the offense was carried out against demands vengeance, I appear and provide the means to that end."

Raptor took a deep breath as he considered what Retribution had just told him. Then he said, "So, you are a celestial being who provides those who demand revenge the means to exact that vengeance?" He looked toward the grotesque figure of Johnson's body fused with the two dogs. "I take it Torrol died at the hands of the man who ran this operation." He looked at the cage in the middle of the warehouse to see the dismembered body of Paul Audrey laying on the floor. "It looks like Audrey is already dead. Isn't he the man who Torrol desired vengeance against? Shouldn't Torrol's quest be over?"

He pointed at the monster in front of him and said, "Also, why turn Torrol into a monster like that? The other instances you spoke of could have been explained by the acts of humans or some other natural phenomena. Why make something so elaborate as a walking corpse with dog parts intermingled into it?"

Retribution smiled and replied, "The vengeance this creature desires has not yet been satiated. Torrol and the dogs not only blame Mr. Audrey for their deaths and the pain they endured. They also blame the people who paid money and cheered as they died."

"As for why I merged Torrol with the two dogs? That is a much simpler answer. I have become quite fond of the movies you humans create. I find the horror genre in particular appealing. The idea of a reanimated corpse grabbing a knife and slashing to pieces those that slashed him to pieces adds a much more personal touch to the act of vengeance. In the past, Nemesis would never have let me create something so brazen as this creature, but with the appearance of people like you and your super-powered allies, the arrival of an undead monster is no longer seen as something out of the realm of possibility. Now stand aside so that Torrol and the dogs may have their vengeance."

Raptor shook his head. "I can't let that happen." He gestured to the dozen bodies ripped to shreds on the floor around him. "Too many people have already died. I will bring the people who were supporting this dog fighting ring to justice. They will serve jail time for what they have done, but I can't allow this senseless killing to go on."

Retribution sighed and retorted, "The universe does not care about justice. Justice is an ideal only recently created by man. The desire for revenge is a powerful emotion that was placed in humans by Nemesis herself. Justice is a human attempt to rationalize one's actions. Vengeance is a divine decree. I am sure you understand why one supersedes the other." Retribution shrugged. "If you are going to stand in the way of vengeance, then vengeance will have to go through you. Now step aside so he may track down and slay those you allowed to escape. This is your one and only warning."

Raptor looked back at the malformed demon that had once been Torrol Johnson. The monster waited for Retribution to nod, then it charged Raptor. The vigilante held his arm out and fired one of the projectiles from his gauntlets. A thick baton struck the zombified horror in the chest and once again sent thousands of volts of electricity surging through its body. The creature's body lit up as the arcs of energy danced around it while its hair stood straight up, and all three heads howled in pain. As the monster was still shaking from the high voltage attack, Raptor hit it with a thrust kick to the chest that caused the beast to fall onto his back.

As the creature was trying to stand back up, Raptor grabbed one of the sphere's attached to his chest and threw it at the monster. When the sphere was halfway between the hero and the beast, the sphere split into two halves connected by a thick cord. The bolas hit the monster and the halves of the sphere wrapped themselves around the three-headed nightmare, ensnaring it tightly in the cord.

The hybrid flexed its ten arms and snapped the military grade cord wrapped around it as if it were paper. The beast then charged Raptor once again and slashed at him with its eight claws.

Raptor used his arms and gauntlets to block the blows and while his armor prevented the claws from cutting him open; each blow the creature delivered nevertheless felt to the vigilante as if he was being hit with a sledgehammer. It was obvious from the feats of strength the creature had displayed that whatever Retribution did to this undead being had greatly increased the strength of the original beings it was formed from.

Through the barrage of scratches and bite attempts Raptor managed to connect with an uppercut to what had been Torrol Johnson's jaw. The blow snapped the monster's middle head back and caused it to back away. With a little more distance between himself and the beast he was fighting, Raptor was able to see the numerous bullet wounds that riddled its body.

He was considering the implications of those gaping wounds when Retribution floated alongside of him and whispered into his ear. "You are right, those bullet holes were put there after Johnson was merged with the two dogs. You are also right in that you have now twice hit my creation with enough electricity to incapacitate even a very large man. You are starting to wonder if fully dismembering my creation will stop it from achieving its vengeance."

Raptor dove at the monster's legs and tackled it to the ground as he wondered if Retribution was either very skilled in observing people and determining what they were thinking or if she was actually reading his mind.

Raptor used each of his fists to simultaneously punch both dog heads in the face as Retribution leaned down next to his helmet. "A little from column A and a little from column B."

Raptor turned to look at the enigmatic woman, which allowed the dog beast to strike him in the ribs. The blow was so powerful that it sent the vigilante tumbling across the floor. Raptor picked himself up off the floor to see his undead enemy making its way toward the hole in the wall that had formerly been the front door.

Raptor quickly stood up and fired another baton from his left gauntlet. This rod had another thick cord attached to it that wrapped around the monster's body. Raptor dug his feet into the floor and pulled hard on the cord in an attempt to keep the beast from leaving the building and seeking out more victims. Despite the hero's augmented strength and increased weight, the monster continued to walk forward as if it was totally unhampered.

Retribution once again floated close to Raptor. "Give it up, hero. Torrol is going to exact revenge on those people who paid to watch him die. He is going to rip them to shreds and there is nothing you can do to stop him."

Raptor considered what Retribution was saying and that was when he realized his mistake in how he was trying to stop this creature.

The vigilante looked over at the phantom-like girl and snarled, "I'm more than just a guy who beats the crap out of criminals. Unlike you, I try to make a real difference in the world."

He then glanced back at the creature in front of him and shouted, "Torrol, listen to me! Remember you were once a criminal! You once sold women like

31

they were property and distributed narcotics to people who were at the lowest points in their lives! How many people died because of your actions? How many of the girls you pimped out caught a disease that killed them? How many of the people you sold drugs to overdosed on your product? Did those people deserve vengeance? Did they deserve to come back as some undead horror and kill you? Or were they better served by justice? Were they better served by you doing your time in jail and then coming out and helping me to stop more crimes, to save more lives?"

Raptor took a deep breath and continued with "Ask yourself, Torrol: were your victims, you, and the people whose lives you helped me save better served by justice or by vengeance?"

The monster stopped walking for a moment, and when Raptor saw a concerned look on Retribution's face, he knew he was making progress.

He started yelling, "Give me a chance, Torrol! Give me a chance to bring those people to justice. Give me a chance to turn them into people who can someday help others to make up for their crimes instead of dying for them."

Retribution floated over to the creature and said, "Those people paid to watch you die! They cheered as you were ripped to pieces! As all three of you were ripped to pieces!"

Tears formed in Johnson's eyes as the dog heads on his two shoulders began to bark and bare their teeth.

The monster turned around and looked at Raptor as he shouted, "Justice! Bring them to justice! I ended my life as a good man and I want to remain that way in death!"

Retribution frowned. "Sorry, Torrol, but the dogs don't care for justice. They still want revenge for what was done to them."

Torrol Johnson looked at the two heads on either side as he screamed, "No! No! I won't be this monster anymore!"

The two dog heads turned to Johnson and began biting into his face. Johnson screamed in pain as his human hands reached up and grabbed one of the dog heads. He ripped the canine head off his shoulder and tossed it to the ground. As the human portion of the undead creature did this, the dog head on his other shoulder tore the nose off his human face.

The remaining dog head then sank his teeth into Johnson's eyes. The young man's head screamed as he was viciously blinded, but still managed to wrap his fingers around the canine's head. With the last of his strength Johnson pulled the dog's head while its teeth were still sunk into his face, this resulted in both his human head and the remaining canine head being yanked off the monstrous cadaver. As the two craniums hit the ground both they and the body they were connected to stopped moving.

Retribution floated over the remains of the nightmare she had created. She looked down at the body parts below her and then at Raptor before speaking. "You may have stopped me from gaining vengeance on the patrons of this place, but your city is a cesspool. Your efforts to stop crime have done little to slow the murder, rape, and other depravities that occur in Port City. "She gestured out the opening in the wall. "Nemesis herself sent me here and I will answer her directive. The victims of Port City will have vengeance for the crimes committed against them."

Raptor took a step closer to Retribution. "The people of Port City will have justice and they will be the better off for it. You on the other hand are finished in this city."

Retribution laughed, "Me, finished? Go ahead take your best shot," she challenged.

Raptor grabbed a sphere from his bandoliers and threw at the phantom's feet. A cloud of liquid nitrogen covered Retribution, freezing everything below and around her, but the spirit herself remained unharmed. Next, Raptor hurled a sphere that exploded in front of Retribution engulfing the entire front half of the warehouse in flames. As the explosion died down, the wall behind Retribution was covered in flames but she was unaffected by the fire.

Raptor was glaring at Retribution as she floated closer to him. "I am a celestial being," she said, "with powers and purpose that you cannot even begin to comprehend. Vengeance has come to Port City, and there's nothing you can do to stop it."

Raptor looked down at what was left of the revenant that had just torn itself apart. "I was able to stop that thing from committing any more murders."

Retribution replied "You had a personal connection with one of my creations. You used that to make a pathetic plea to him. Unfortunately, he bought into your whining and thus robbed all three of those creatures and me of revenge."

The higher being smiled and continued with. "That will not be so easy with the other creation I made." She looked at the city. "Or, with the creations I am still going to make." She turned and smiled at Raptor. "I like to be there when those who require my services are wronged. It really helps me to empathize with their plight and understand why they want personal vengeance as opposed to impartial justice."

Retribution waved adieu at Raptor as she said, "Goodbye, Ben Watkins. Have fun chasing down and trying to stop my next slasher. His hit list is quite long and spread out across the city. When you catch up with him, I will meet you there to watch as you try in vain to stop him. While I do not want to see you get hurt, I do enjoy the theatrics of your trying to defeat a creature far more powerful than you."

Retribution winked and then she was gone, leaving Raptor standing in a burning building with a pile of corpses.

Raptor looked around for a moment until he heard sirens coming his way. He quickly exited the building and mounted his motorcycle.

As he was driving away, the vigilante gave a command into his visor. "Drone, return to base. Computer, find me all the information, myths, and legends you can about vengeance spirits." The hero shook his head and muttered to himself, "If she is as powerful as she appears to be this city could be looking at a slew of murders coming our way."

CHAPTER 5

Coach Ken Flanagan was in his office with his assistant coach. The two were watching videos of several new possible recruits to bring to his team next season. Both men cheered as they watched a young man who was over seven feet tall turn around and dunk on a player who was absolutely over matched by the giant he was guarding.

Flanagan turned around to his assistant and said, "That's a big boy. His skills are a little raw, though; he could use some help with passing out of the post and rotating some on defense."

The assistant coach nodded and replied, "True, but you can't teach size and power like that."

"You're right," Flanagan concurred. "If we can land this guy, we would easily have the best young front court in the conference."

His assistant smiled. "Yeah, with Charles graduating we're going to need to rebuild the front court."

At the mention of Charles' name, Flanagan quickly changed the topic. "Yeah, let's put the full press on this seven-footer. We're going to offer him a full scholarship, bring him out here, and have some of our cheerleaders with the most school spirit come out to meet him." Flanagan chuckled at the last comment, as did his assistant coach. He then looked at his watch. "Speaking of special guests, I've got one coming over in a few minutes, so I need you to get going. If my wife happens to ask you about me, tell her we were here till after midnight watching videos on recruits."

The assistant coach raised his hand in agreement, "You got it, coach. I'll see you tomorrow morning." With that said, the assistant coach left the office and made his way to his car.

Coach Flanagan quickly fixed his hair and brushed his teeth. He then went to his desk and pulled out a large wad of cash he had scored in his latest point shaving endeavor. He heard a knock on his door, and he opened it to see a woman with long black hair wearing a halter top and fishnet stockings standing there.

The coach smiled. "Trixie, I missed you, babe."

The prostitute smiled back and replied. "Hey, coach. I missed you too, and so did the friend you asked me to bring."

Flanagan raised his eyebrows "Is your friend here?"

Trixie shifted her mouth into suggestive shape "She's not here yet, but if you've got the money, I told you to bring, I'll text her and she'll be here in a few minutes."

Flanagan waved the cash he had taken out of his desk in front of Trixie. "I've got the cash for you, your friend, and a little extra for a tip if things work out the way I hope."

Trixie slightly tilted her head so that her loose-fitting shirt slid farther down her shoulder. "Well then, I'll text my friend, but since you have extra cash for a tip why don't you and I get started and we'll see if I can get that tip out of you before my friend gets here."

She grabbed Flanagan's tie and started leading him toward the large couch at the back of his office.

Outside of Flanagan's office, a large gray hand reached up from the bottom of a storm drain and wrapped its hand around the grating. With a single shove, the hand pushed the grate off its foundation and threw it onto the sidewalk. The hand then reached out of the drain and grabbed the curb. With one pull a tall, well built, soaking wet body with a potato sack over its head rose out of the gutter.

The figure turned toward Flanagan's office so that the holes cut in the sack were looking at the coach's window. The hulking figure looked to his left to see Retribution floating above the sidewalk next to him.

The spirit of vengeance smiled at the revenant. "I told you that I would help you out," the spirit of vengeance said to the revenant. "The first person who cost you your life, who betrayed and drowned you, is right inside that office. This is your chance to get revenge for what he did to you."

The revenant groaned once more and then started walking toward the building.

Inside the building, Andrew McGown was sitting at his security guard post and thinking about what he was going to do with the money Coach Flanagan had given him for letting the prostitute into the building. He was thinking about making a trip to a nearby strip club where some of the college girls he saw on campus worked at night to earn income to pay for their classes. He was trying to figure out how many dances he could buy when he saw a huge man with a potato sack over his head walking toward the building.

As the man approached the building, McGown stood up from his desk and sighed. He hoped the guy would just turn and go to some other edifice but when he approached the door to his building, McGown knew that he was going to have to deal with the guy.

As the hulking figure walked into the door, the stench coming off the giant forced McGown to take several steps back. "Jesus, you smell!" He took a closer look at the person and noticed that his clothes were soaking wet. "Look, I don't know if this is some kind of a frat prank or whatever, but you need to get out of here!"

The brute ignored McGown and started walking down the hallway toward Flanagan's office. Seeing that the figure was not listening to him, McGown stood up and grabbed the large man by the arm. The sack-headed man turned to look at McGown then pushed him to the ground with enough force to send the security guard sliding into the wall. The bag-headed man took a brief look at McGown before resuming his trek toward Flanagan's office.

The guard grabbed his baton as he cursed, "Damn it! That's it! No more playing around!"

McGown rushed up and struck the giant in the back of the head with such force that he shattered his baton. The mysterious figure's head shifted forward, but he was otherwise unaffected by the blow. The brute slowly turned around, grabbed McGown by the throat, lifted him into the air, and then threw him into the wall. The security man hit the partition so hard that he smashed through the drywall covering and into the cinder blocks behind it. The unconscious guard slid down the wall and fell onto the floor in a heap.

The revenant that had been Charles Donner looked to his left to see Retribution standing there. She gestured toward the emergency case on the other side of the wall.

"Grab the axe. Make him feel the fear you felt as you drifted down to the bottom of the water."

The revenant grunted again and smashed the glass containing the fire axe. He then turned his head back in the direction of Flanagan's office and once more started walking toward it.

Flanagan was engaged with Trixie on the couch when there was a loud banging on his door.

The coach looked down at the prostitute and queried, "Why in the hell is your friend knocking on the door so loudly? Does she want the entire campus to know what's going on in here?"

The second bang on the door was even louder. Flanagan sighed. "Jesus, what is she, built like a linebacker to be hitting the door that hard?" He pulled himself off Trixie. "I better go answer that before I have to pay off another security guard."

Flanagan was walking toward the entrance and pulling up his pants when the door suddenly exploded inward in a maelstrom of splintered wood, glass, and steel. The coach tumbled backwards and fell to the floor as the hulking figure of the revenant that had been Charles Donner lumbered into his office wielding an axe.

The dead man walked farther into the room until he was standing over his former coach. Charles shifted the potato sack that was over his head so that Flanagan could see his rage filled eyes as he looked down at the mentor who had betrayed him.

Trixie screamed and tried to run for the door. As she was running past him, Charles shot out his hand and grabbed her by the throat. He effortlessly lifted the prostitute off the ground and bellowed at her. He did not wish to kill the young woman, but he also did not want her to run for help and alert others to his presence. The zombified student threw the hooker into the wall, knocking her unconscious.

As Trixie was sliding down the wall Flanagan tried to run past Charles. The coach had almost reached the door when the undead former athlete drove his axe into the back of Flanagan's left leg. The corrupt coach fell to the floor screaming in pain as blood spurted out of his leg to cover the walls and carpet in scarlet.

Flanagan was crying as he rolled over and screamed, "Don't kill me! I have money! I can pay! Whatever it is, I can pay!"

Charles reached up and pulled the potato sack off his head to reveal his face.

A wave of terror ran down Flanagan's spine as he looked at the gray, bloated visage of his former power forward.

Flanagan started shaking his head. "No. No. You can't be here. You're dead! The Barracuda killed you! You should be at the bottom of the bay!"

When Charles opened his mouth to respond salt water seeped out of it. "He killed me on your word, Coach! You condemn me to drown to death to protect your point shaving scheme!" The slasher turned his head toward the unconscious form of Trixie. "You let them murder me so that you could continue to get money to buy hookers with?"

Flanagan shook his head and pleaded, "It's not like that. You were point shaving too. You got greedy and you tried to beat the system. You tried to double cross the Barracuda." The coach started to nod. "Yeah, that's it. The Barracuda! He... he's the one that had you killed. It's him you should be after, not me! He's the guy who calls the shots! He's the one that deserves to die!"

Charles pointed his axe at Flanagan. "I trusted you! I trusted you to help me through college! To help me become a man! I made mistakes, but did I deserve to die for them? Did I deserve for you to sell me out to the Barracuda?"

Charles shook his head, sending flecks of salt water and seaweed that was stuck in his hair flying all over Flanagan's office. "No! I deserved better and you deserve to die for what you have done!"

Charles brought the axe crashing down into his former coach's other leg. Flanagan screamed in pain as his blood shot out over his office. The enraged revenant then took a half step forward and drove the hatchet blade into the coach's right hip. He swung the axe with such force that it shattered Flanagan's hip bone and embedded itself in the floor.

Flanagan was screeching in agony as Charles pulled the axe out of the floor and lifted it over his head again. The coach looked up his undead player and saw Retribution standing next to him.

As the blood continued to pour out of Flanagan's numerous wounds, he could hear the ghostly voice of the spectral figure giving Charles directions. "That's right, work your way up his body. Do not just bury the axe in his head

39

and end his life quickly. You deserve more than a quick death from him. Was your death quick when he helped to drown you? Or was it a long and painful death?" She smiled as she looked down at the coach. "Make him feel every bit of pain that you felt when you were drowning. Make your vengeance worthwhile."

Charles moaned and drove the axe into Flanagan's left hip. Once more the creature struck with enough force to shatter his coach's bones. The monster lifted the axe again and buried it into the right side of Flanagan's rib cage. He repeated the process for the other side of the severely wounded man's ribcage and both of his shoulders. After smashing Flanagan's left shoulder to pieces, he looked into his coach's eyes.

Flanagan looked up through tear-filled eyes. His body was wracked with unbelievable pain and he was bleeding to death. The corrupt coach again tried pleading with his former player. "It hurts so bad. Please just end it. End the pain for me."

Charles leaned down over his coach, and as he spoke to him more salt water seeped out of his mouth and onto Flanagan's face. "The water wasn't quick with me. It was a slow and painful death. Just like yours will be."

Charles then rested his blood-soaked axe over his shoulder, pulled the potato sack back over his head, and walked out of the office.

Retribution floated over to Flanagan and looked down at the man as he breathed his last pain-filled breath. "You have suffered Retribution. When you arrive in Hell tell them that it was me who sent you there."

Flanagan screamed one more time as Retribution's beautiful face faded into nothing but a skull, and her stunning eyes became dark black pits. As Flanagan's scream ended so did his life. With the vile coach dead, Retribution looked toward the window to see Charles standing above the storm drain he had crawled out of. In the blink of an eye, she was on the street floating just off the ground next to him.

Charles then climbed back down into the storm drain, reached out from the sewer, grabbed the grating he had dislodged, and pulled it back into place.

As the slasher was making his way back down the storm drain, Retribution called out to him. 'What are we doing next, hunting or fishing?"

Charles replied in his garbled voice, "The Moose dies next!"

Retribution smiled. "Hunting it is, then."

After that, Retribution simply disappeared into the wind.

CHAPTER 6

The sun rose as Ben Watkins sat in his office and stared at his computer screen. After his escapades as Raptor the previous night, he had gone home and gotten roughly three hours sleep. Watkins knew he needed a few more hours sleep to keep his body functioning at peak condition. He decided that he would leave the office early and grab a few hours of sleep before he returned to the streets as Raptor.

For now, his attention was focused on two items that occupied his computer screen. One object of his attention was a report of Ken Flanagan, the head basketball coach at Port City University, being murdered in his office last night. Flanagan was in his office when, according to reports from both a security guard and a prostitute on the scene, a huge man with a sack over his head walked into the building, knocked out the guard and the prostitute, and then axed Flanagan to death.

Given the damage to Flanagan's body and the strength reportedly exhibited by the murderer, Watkins felt as if this case could be another example of Retribution creating a revenant. Watkins sighed and shook his head in frustration. If Retribution was truly going to stay in his city, then he could be looking at a rash of these types of murders occurring. One thing Retribution was right about was that Port City was a cesspool full of criminals and murders. Despite the best efforts of Raptor and the police force, Port City still had one of the highest murder rates in the U.S. Since he had started operating as Raptor the murder rate had gone down noticeably, but it was still much higher than many other cities in the country.

The truth of the matter was that if Retribution was looking for murder victims to turn into undead vengeful corpses there would be no shortage of candidates to choose from in Port City. For a brief moment, the hero wondered if an initial increase from the murders committed by the revenants would cause the overall murder rate in the city to drop. After a few murderers were slain, would the rest of the city start to realize what was going on and restrain themselves from committing murder themselves?

Watkins scolded himself for even considering the idea and then pushed it aside. He reminded himself that the Torrol/dog creature he fought last night was determined to slaughter the spectators who were watching the dog fights. Clearly, Retribution was not a being who was concerned about the punishment fitting the crime.

Watkins made a mental note to look into whatever Coach Flanagan was involved with that could have made him a target of Retribution and one of her revenants. Just as Paul Audrey was not the only target of Torrol and the dogs, Flanagan was likely only the first victim of a second revenant.

Watkins then turned his attention to the other information on his computer screen. The mini-supercomputer in his visor had been working all night compiling data on Retribution and other spirits of vengeance. He had recalled that one of the names Retribution had referred to herself as was Poena. His algorithm had numerous articles on the mythological deity, and he was now reviewing that information.

It seemed that Poena was the personified spirit of retribution, vengeance, recompense, punishment, and penalty for the crime of murder and manslaughter. A derivative of her name was also used to describe the money paid to the family of a murder victim to expiate the crime.

One of the other names Retribution had referred to herself as was Adrestia, whose name translated into "She Who Cannot be Escaped." In this instance, she was the daughter of the gods of love and war and was associated with Nemesis, the Goddess of Vengeance. Due to her attributes and abilities, she was often fought over by gods and titans to recruit her to their various agendas.

Watkins nodded and said to himself, "I suppose if you are going to war, having someone on your side who can bring back the dead with an insatiable desire to kill those who wronged them would certainly help to tip the scales in your favor."

The third name that she referred to herself was Praxidice. In this instance, Praxidice was the spirit of judicial punishment and vengeance. Watkins took out his pen and wrote down the terms "judicial punishment" and "vengeance." Retribution was quick to discount his suggestion to her that justice was preferable to vengeance. He did a quick search for how the two concepts were perceived in ancient Greek and Roman culture. His search revealed that in those cultures judicial punishment and vengeance were often intertwined, with the distinction between the two being vague at best.

After looking over the same information five times, the fine line between judicial punishment and vengeance was all he could find as an approach to Retribution. With all the information his algorithm could find on the names Retribution had given him there was no instance of weakness or a way to attack her. None of the names she had given to Raptor came up with a mythical hero or weapon that had managed to harm or even to defeat Retribution in any of her guises.

Raptor took a deep breath as he considered the fact that he may be facing a threat that there was nothing he could do to stop. The hero was forced to come to terms that he was a man fighting against a god.

He was about to attempt another research endeavor for anything that would give him an advantage over Retribution when there was a knock on his door.

Watkins closed out his computer and said, "Come in."

The door opened and Chester Mansfield peered into the office. "Mr. Watkins, I was hoping I could have a few more minutes of your time."

Watkins took a deep breath and replied, "Sure, Chester. Come on in."

Mansfield walked into the office and was halfway to Watkins' desk, when the latter stood up and walked across the room.

When Ben reached his employee, he held out his hand. "Chester, I owe you an apology. The other day when we were discussing possible military contracts, I intimidated you and spoke down to you in front of your peers. As you know that is a touchy subject for me, but that's not an excuse to behave as I did. Acting that way was unprofessional of me and I wanted to let you know that I am truly sorry about it. At the next board meeting, I will make a public apology as well."

"Thanks, Mr. Watkins. I accept your apology." Mansfield took a step back and looked away from his employer. "I hope that in light of your apology, I can attempt to bring up the subject of military contracts with you one more time."

He pulled a flash drive out of his pocket and attempted to hand it to Watkins. "If you could just review this data, I've compiled with projections about the amount of profits we could make with military contracts, along with riders we could put into the contracts to address some of your fears about how our technology will be utilized."

Watkin's face was flush with anger, but he took a deep breath and calmed himself down. "Chester, I appreciate your dedication to this company, the hard work you have put into this project, and your courage for coming to me again. However, I will again tell you that I will block any attempts for our technology to fall into military hands. For the last time, I will not discuss this matter with you or anyone else again." He looked calmly into Mansfield's face before continuing. "Now, please put this idea to rest and focus on other areas that we can expand into."

Mansfield was visibly shaking as he looked at the owner and CEO of his company. "Mr. Watkins, if you could just look at the data, I have compiled I would be happy to show all of the positive…"

Watkins held up his hand and gave Mansfield a stern look. "Chester, after the way I acted at the board meeting, I am trying very hard to maintain my professionalism right now, but you are testing me. Let this go, Chester. Let this idea go and look into something else that you can focus on."

Chester was sweating and swallowed hard as he looked into Watkins' eyes. "If you would only…"

Watkins cut him off. "Chester, either drop this idea or clean out your desk. I can't make my stance on this subject any clearer than that. Do you understand what I am saying?"

Mansfield nodded. "Yes, Mr. Watkins. Thank you for your time." He turned and walked toward the door. "Have a good day, sir"

Watkins kept staring at Mansfield as he walked out. "You have a good day too, Chester."

As his employee departed, Watkins went back to his computer.

He looked at the screen for a moment and then started thinking out loud again. "Searching for information on the Web is only scratching the surface of the information I need." He gave a verbal command to his computer: "Find me an expert in mythology and folklore in Port City." The computer which Watkins had linked to Raptor's visor began searching.

Outside of the office, Mansfield took out his cell phone and quickly typed in a text message: *"I tried one last time, but Watkins won't go for the military contract."*

Mansfield continued to sweat as he saw the dots on his phone, and he waited for the response. After what seemed like an eternity, the reply finally came through: *We need to talk face to face. Meet us tonight 9pm at the usual place.*

Mansfield sighed as he put his phone back into his pocket and wiped his forehead clear of the puddle of sweat that had formed on it.

CHAPTER 7

It was around 8pm as Raptor used the shadows to creep into Port City University. As he stepped onto the campus grounds, he gave a command to his visor, "Activate exo-suit stealth mode."

The command caused a black ripple to roll over Raptor's suit, helmet, and cape. While the hero would be visible to the naked eye, his image would appear as nothing more than a mirage-like distortion on the university's security cameras.

The hero then silently moved into the office of the murdered Coach Flanagan. The masked gumshoe had read the police report on the murder, but he needed to take a closer look at the crime scene himself. As a detective, Raptor knew that above all else he needed to avoid confirmation bias when conducting an investigation. When reviewing the information in the police report the evidence suggested that Coach Flanagan's death was the result of an attack by one of Retribution's revenants. Given the threat that Retribution presented she needed to be his first priority.

If the coach was murdered by one of Retribution's monsters, Raptor knew he would have to act quickly to determine where the revenant who murdered Flanagan went. Considering how the Torrol/pit bull hybrid had determined that everyone in the warehouse who was betting on fights deserved to die, there was a good chance that if a revenant had killed Flanagan, the undead creature would now be on the hunt for other victims.

These facts made it all the more important for Raptor to review the crime scene without the specific intent of finding data that would support the idea the slaying was committed by a resurrected murder victim. If the data led him to that conclusion, then this murder would move to the near the top of his priority list. If the data suggested the homicide was more mundane, he would still catalog what he had found and share it with the police.

If they did not solve the murder while he was dealing with Retribution, he would look into the matter after dealing with the more immediate threat. For now, however, his focus had to be on the vengeful goddess that had entered his city. In order to deal with her, the crime fighter had to make sure he wasn't making up false leads to get to her.

The first thing Raptor looked at were the axe wounds in the floor where the murderer supposedly cut through the coach's bone and into the floor with a single swing. The hero bent down and looked at the grooves where the blade had been driven into the subfloor. Each of the grooves was relatively smooth and they were fairly symmetrical. It was clear that the blows were indeed from one strike each and not multiple blows to the same area.

The hero then activated the visual enhancement function on his visor. While the visor was not able to examine things on a microscopic level, it was still able to greatly magnify whatever Raptor was looking at. As the vigilante peered into the first groove, he saw little pieces of blood and covered bone. The next two grooves revealed similar results. Raptor stood and gave a command to his visor, "Start recording."

The grooves in the floor were indeed made by a single strike. The presence of bone fragments and blood confirm that both bone and floor were cut through with a single blow. Strength of this magnitude could only have been generated by a superhuman or an individual wearing a strength enhancing exo-suit."

Raptor then moved onto the odd discolorations on the floor. The hero scraped up several samples. Most of them he stored in an empty sphere on his bandoliers. He also took one sample, lifted it up to his visor, and brought it to his nose.

He sniffed the sample and then continued his narration, "Discoloration on the floor has the visual appearance and odor of stains recently created by exposure to salt water. Analysis back in the lab will be needed to fully confirm this hypothesis."

Raptor then moved over to the wall and examined it through the enhanced viewing application of his visor. He noticed several green streaks on the wall. He again scraped off samples, sniffed one of them, and placed the rest in another evidence sphere on his bandoliers.

Once the samples were secure, he started recording again. "Samples on the wall have the visual appearance and odor of seaweed. These samples will also be reviewed in the lab to confirm. End recording"

Raptor then walked over to the Flanagan's computer and turned it on. He used an HDMI cable to connect the coach's computer to his visor. Once his visor indicated that it had established a connection with the university's Internet server, he gave another command: "Access university security cameras."

A message flashed across his visor saying, *Bypassing firewalls.* Within ten seconds, Raptor's program had full access to the college's security camera. The vigilante then ordered his visor to bring up the feed for the building he was in at the time of the murder.

The video showed a large man with pale skin and a potato sack over his head walking into the building. Raptor paused the video and took a close look at the man's arms and hands.

He then spoke into his visor, "Record. The assailant's skin appears to be pale and pruned as if he has been submerged in water for an extended period. He appears to be around '6'5" and in peak physical condition."

Raptor watched as the assailant got into an altercation with a security guard, where the assailant shook off a blow from the sentry's baton and threw him into the wall. This verified that the accoster had superhuman strength as he was clearly not wearing an exo-suit.

The last thing to catch Raptor's attention was when the assailant seemed to stop moving and looked at the area to his left as if he were listening to someone. He then turned and took the fire axe off the wall.

Raptor sighed and started recording again. "The assailant seems to be taking direction from an individual who does not appear on the recording. There is no visual distortion in the area, likely ruling out an individual wearing an exo-suit in stealth mode. This could indicate either psychosis or the presence of a being who does not appear in the visual spectrum. While the forensic evidence will have still be tested, initial findings suggest this murder was committed by one of Retribution's revenants.

"After interviewing Vergil Knight on the other side of the campus, the next suggested course of action should be to investigate the murders or disappearances of a '6'5" man associated with Ken Flanagan, possibly a member from his basketball team. The focus of the investigation should be potential drowning victims which could point to organized crime rings."

The hero took a deep breath before continuing with, "If a revenant is going after a criminal organization the body count racked up by this creature could quickly become very high. Additionally, depending on where and when the revenant engages the members of the organization, civilian casualties could become a factor as well. End recording."

Raptor looked at the time and said to himself, "Only five minutes until Professor Knight finishes his next class. I have to hurry if I am going to catch him before he enters his car."

The vigilante moved out of the hallway and then left through the building's fire door. As he exited the building, he saw two stray security guards coming his way. Not wanting to waste time engaging with the guards, Raptor slid behind a nearby dumpster and waited for the sentries to walk by. He then moved between the shadows of trees, buildings, and other outcroppings as he made his way to the Social Sciences Building. Once he found the window looking into Room 616, he stopped and crouched down behind the cover of a large tree. He then watched and waited for the class to end.

Vergil Knight's bad leg was bothering him. The pain forced the professor to lean on his cane as he stood up and walked to the front of his classroom. There was a particularly voluptuous young woman sitting in the front row and today she was wearing an unusually tight shirt. The professor positioned himself in a spot where he could look at the college student at just the right angle, without making it too obvious that he was checking her out.

As he stood in front of the class, he caught himself standing silently for a moment too long as he was doing his best to not be caught ogling the young woman. What Vergil Knight was unaware of was that as he was staring at his student, someone else was staring at him from the shadows outside of his window.

Vergil cleared his throat to help refocus himself and quickly looked to the back of the class in an attempt to obscure what he had really been doing. He fixed his eyes on another attractive young woman sitting against the back wall and then resumed his lecture.

"So, it is with the story of *The Odyssey*, and the wit of Odysseus, that we complete our section of this class on Greek and Roman mythology."

He grabbed a book off his desk and held it up. "For next week's class, we will be moving into Eastern mythology. We will begin this section by reading the 16th century novel *Journey to the West*!" He shifted his eyes back to the attractive girl in the front row and said, "I know what you're thinking. It's kind of funny that we are starting our section on Eastern mythology with a book called a *Journey to the West*."

The student he had leaned into rolled her eyes at the dad joke her professor had just dropped.

Vergil shrugged and leaned back on his cane. "Does anyone know what this book is about?"

He noticed that most of his students were looking at the clock and counting down the seconds until they could leave their elective class. He sighed and continued on. "It's the story of Sun Wukong, The Monkey King, The Great Sage Equal to Heaven!"

Vergil looked over the crowd still seeing that he had managed to capture absolutely none of the students' interest.

With only three minutes left before the class was over, the frustrated professor pulled out the one thing that he knew would catch the attention of at least some of his students. He looked to the small group of young men who always sat against the right-hand side of the wall underneath the defunct chalkboard. Predictably, one of them was wearing an Evangelion shirt, one a My Hero Academia Shirt, and one Gundam shirt.

Vergil took a few steps in their direction as he said, "Has anyone ever heard of the anime cartoon *Dragon Ball Z?*"

The anime trio, as Vergil referred to them in his head, suddenly perked up and looked in his direction. Vergil smiled as he held *Journey to the West* above his head.

"The character known as Sun Goku is heavily inspired by Sun Wukong. In fact, that's why Son Goku has his monkey tail. Also, Goku's ability to change, his magic staff, nimbus cloud, and ridiculous power levels are all taken directly from Sun Wukong's story. The first act of the book with Sun Wukong warring against gods and monsters is almost exactly like an anime movie."

The anime trio were suddenly nodding their heads excitedly to engage in this new section of his class. With only a minute left before he had to dismiss his students, Vergil hobbled back to his desk and slid his chair slightly to the right, so he could see the door.

He then said, "All right, that's it for today. I look forward to seeing you all next week."

Vergil then sat down so he was eye level with the female students' backsides as they walked out of class. After the students had cleared out, the professor tried his best to stretch out his aching leg and then he started to make his way out to his car. It was nearly nine o'clock and most of the campus was empty.

Aside from the fact that the majority of the students shied away from night classes, most of them who lived on campus had stayed indoors given the fact that the university's head basketball coach was murdered the previous night. When he heard the news, Vergil thought for a minute that the Dean might cancel classes for the day, but that call never came.

The adjunct professor shrugged as he was walking across the empty parking lot toward his car as he mused to himself, "Oh, well. I guess if they canceled class every time there was a murder in Port City, we'd never have classes."

Vergil had almost reached his car when a gruff voice called out to him from a nearby tree. "Mr. Knight."

Vergil turned around and saw Raptor standing behind them. The professor started shaking and stuttering when he saw the vigilante, "Ya ...ya ...you're him. Ya ...ya... you're Raptor!"

Raptor moved out from the shadows and closer to Vergil, "Yes, and I need your help."

Vergil was stunned at the request. "My help?" he replied. "You need my help? I mean, you're like a real modern version of a mythical hero. You're like Achilles, or Theseus, or Perseus. I mean, you've, like literally fought dragons!"

"Yes, and I now, I need your help to combat a threat that I don't understand, but you might."

"Okay, go ahead and let me hear it."

Raptor gestured toward a nearby bench. "Will it do your leg better to sit down?"

Vergil shook his head. "No, actually if I am standing the blood flow is a little better and helps my leg. As long as I can lean on my cane, I'll be fine. Please go on, though. I'm dying to see if I can help out a real-life hero on his journey."

"Very well. I have recently come into conflict with a being calling herself Retribution. She claims to be a goddess of vengeance sent here at the behest of what she referred to as 'the aspect of what we think of as God that we would call Nemesis.' She also claimed to have been known by various other names throughout history such as Adrestia, Praxidice, and Poena.

51

"I can attest to the fact that her powers are vast. She was unfazed by most of my arsenal. She is able to hide her presence from humans. Most importantly, she has the ability to raise the dead and turn them into extremely powerful revenants like something from a horror movie. She is resurrecting people who have recently been murdered and sending them after those they believe are responsible for their deaths.

"I can't abide that under any circumstances. To make matters worse, the concept of who is responsible for the death of the revenant seems to be a very loosely defined term. As such, the number of people they are murdering can be very high. I tried to research the names Retribution gave me using the Internet, but I couldn't find any accounts of heroes stopping her, or even attempting to challenge her. I was hoping that you might have some insight into how I could approach this being."

Vergil was rocking back and forth on his cane. "I mean, I know monsters and supervillains are real just based on what I've seen on the news, oftentimes involving you -- but now actual gods and goddesses? That's really something."

He shrugged before continuing. "Well, if she is Poena, she's pretty much the right hand of Nemesis. Her name would mean pain, punishment, or penalty. It would make sense if Poena was currently calling herself Retribution. Nemesis herself predominantly dealt with crimes of a divine matter such as when Narcissus rejected the advances of the nymph Echo due to his vanity. Something like human-on-human crime she would probably pass onto Poena or Retribution as she is currently calling herself."

Raptor nodded in understanding. "So, this seems to confirm her identity but still doesn't tell me how I can stop her."

"That's the thing, though. In myth, Poena was never stopped. Myths of her history are a little scattered. Sometimes she is represented as always having been a divine being. Other myths indicated she was at one time a human who was endowed with godlike powers by Nemesis. Whatever her origin was, she was righteous vengeance; she was the good guy, so she never lost." He gestured toward Raptor, "In the eyes of the Ancient Greeks and Romans, she was *you*. She gave evil doers what they deserved."

Raptor held up his hands. "I bring justice to those who commit crimes, not vengeance. I also don't hand out punishments; that's for the courts and the people of the city to decide, not a solo individual, be they human or god."

Vergil shrugged again. "I am going to guess that Retribution disagreed with you on the concept of vengeance versus justice?"

Raptor nodded. "I did find one thing in the Praxidice name she had mentioned, though. Praxidice was supposed to be a goddess of judicial punishment and vengeance. I understand that in ancient times the two concepts were nearly indistinguishable, but there is a difference between the two. The question I have for you is: How can I get Retribution to understand that difference?"

Vergil shook his head. "You won't be able to convince her of the difference. In myth, she was the handmaiden of Nemesis. She did whatever Nemesis said without question and without much in-depth thought. Her job was to carry out Nemesis' commands and anything that got in her way be damned."

Vergil could see that Raptor was unhappy with his response, so he tried to rephrase what he was saying. "Try to think of it this way. Poena or Retribution is like the Terminator. The Terminator was programmed by Skynet to kill Sarah Connor and that was its only objective. It didn't matter who else it had to kill along the way as long as it killed Sarah Connor.

"Retribution has been sent by Nemesis to bring vengeance to those who have been wrongfully killed. Hence, she is going to carry out that command without putting too much thought into who else is hurt or killed along the way. If the victim she brings back think multiple people have to die, then multiple people have to die. Like the Terminator, there are no shades of gray with her; there are only the people who those she brings back think are responsible for their deaths and those who they don't."

An idea began to form in Raptor's mind. "If I am unable to stop her physically then the only way to stop her would be to have her reprogrammed?"

Vergil grimaced as he replied. "I mean, possibly, but the only being capable of doing that would be Nemesis herself and getting her attention won't be easy. Let alone convincing her that her handmaiden is acting beyond the scope of her orders. For God sakes, you're talking about an entity that was even feared by Zeus!"

"From what I've read about Nemesis, aside from mainly dealing in matters concerning the divine, and being the embodiment of vengeance, she is also a goddess of equilibrium. If Retribution is dealing out punishments unequal to the crime, then wouldn't she need to interject herself into her servant's actions?"

Vergil grabbed his chin as he pondered his answer before replying. "Possibly, but you'd have to convince her to come and hear your case and that won't be an easy task. I mean, according to myth, you'd be lucky not to die in the process of trying to convince her to come to you."

The professor gave Raptor a concerned look. "Well, first you'd have to do something that was an affront to a divine being."

"I plan to try and stop each and every revenant Retribution brings back."

"Assuming you were able to be enough of a disruption to Retribution for her to consider what you are doing an affront to her divinity and she doesn't kill you herself in the process. You'd then have to use sacred scales -- and before you ask, I don't know what would qualify as such -- but you would have to place two means of dispensing justice on it but traditionally, it's been a sword and whip. And then you recite the following prayer."

Raptor held up his hand. "Hold on." He gave a command to his visor: "Start recording." He then nodded to Vergil. "Go ahead."

Vergil closed his eyes as he began the ancient prayer.

"I praise bright-eyed Nemesis, daughter of dark-cloaked Nyx;

Nemesis who watches, who knows whenever we have done harm, who makes certain that all evil is punished, that all who are guilty receive their due.

Swift-winged Nemesis, bearer of the apple branch, in days of old were you well honored, goddess, by those who suffered the losses and pains of love;

Many were the false-hearted lovers who felt your wrath.

Fair-minded Nemesis, just one, unyielding one, you are the firmest foe of cruel and violent men;

You are the avenger of the wronged, the disperser of right reward.

Nemesis, I honor you."

He opened his eyes as he ended the recitation. "Then it's just a matter of hoping the myths are true."

"Thank you, Mr. Knight."

With that said, the avian crusader disappeared into the darkness.

Vergil shrugged and started walking toward his car. "I guess that's likely to be the most exciting thing that happens to me in my lifetime."

As Raptor was speeding away, he thought about where he could find "divine scales of justice." There was only one set of scales in the city that could be considered divine on top of the city courthouse held aloft by the statue of Lady Justice. If the scales that symbolize justice for an entire city were not divine, then Raptor had no idea what would meet the criteria.

The hero spoke aloud to himself as he drove down the darkened streets of Port City: "The easiest way to get to the scales would be to swing over from the top of the Watkins Building." He smiled. "Looks like I'm going back to work."

The hero turned and started heading to his base of operations.

He gave a command into this visor: "Get the transport ready to return me to the office."

CHAPTER 8

Chester Mansfield crept into the construction site for one of Ben Watkins' new buildings. As a member of the board for Watkins' company, no one really questioned if he visited the site after the construction crews had all left. With that knowledge, Mansfield had set up several meetings with his contact at this location. He figured they could talk without really having to worry about anyone else being around and listening into their conversation.

Work on the building was progressing slowly. The construction crew had the skeletal frame of the structure up as well as the majority of the foundation laid out. As Mansfield looked up at the building he felt as if it was an apropos metaphor for his current situation. In its current state, the facility looked as if it would never be completed. The irony was not lost on Mansfield as it appeared that the contract, he had promised the people he was about meet with looked as if it would never be completed either.

A long black limousine pulled to a stop and three men in black coats exited the vehicle. They opened the back door and a tall man with a crew cut stepped out and stared directly at Mansfield. The man with the crew cut was Special Agent Brain Desopo of the CIA He had been expecting Mansfield to deliver him a military contract that would have armed his people in the field and have brought him a lot of money.

Desopo shook his head in disappointment as he started walking toward Mansfield. At the sight of Desopo and the men accompanying him, Mansfield's knees began to shake, and his brow started perspiring. When Desopo was close to him Mansfield started talking.

"Agent Desopo, I want to reiterate again how sorry I am for not being able to close this deal. I tried as best I could to convince Watkins to sign off on it, but no matter how much money was on the table he wouldn't budge. Perhaps, I can work with the board to try and orchestrate some manner of hostile takeover of the company from Mr. Watkins. I mean, the money we are talking about is substantial."

Desopo held up his hand and replied, "That's never going to happen, Mansfield. You know as well as I do that Ben Watkins has a stranglehold on that company. Even if the company wasn't making money hand over fist there is virtually no way to force Watkins out of his position."

Mansfield shrugged. "Well, I guess there's nothing else we can do, then. We'll just have to put this whole thing behind us and move on, right?"

Desopo reached out and grabbed Mansfield by the shirt. "Wrong, Mansfield! We are far from putting this behind us. I can smooth over things with my superiors at the CIA but there are other people involved. People who you can't smooth things over with. People in other countries who were going to buy some of those weapons from me for a much higher price than we were going to pay Watkins for them!"

He pushed the trembling executive back. "Christ, Mansfield! If you could have done what you promised us you could do, everyone would have won! You would have made a lot of money. Watkins and your board would have made a lot of money. We could have flipped a third of the weapons to our contacts overseas for more than we would have paid for the entire contract. Then those forces would have used the weapons to overthrow regimes who are acting against our interests! Everyone would have come out on top! Now we are all deep in a pile of shit because you couldn't convince your boss to make a goddamn fortune!"

Desopo shook his head before continuing his tirade. "We have to give those guys overseas something, Mansfield. If we don't, they are going to cause a ton of headaches not just for us personally but for our entire country. They were counting on getting those weapons and then modifying them to make them lethal in order to take over a country, for crying out loud!"

"You never said anything about selling the weapons Mr. Watkins had developed to foreign powers." He looked to the sky in disbelief. "My god, Watkins was right. Those weapons would have fallen into the wrong hands.

Raptor: Retribution of the Revenants | Matthew Dennion

They would have fallen into the hands of terrorists, just like the ones that had killed his family."

Desopo struck Mansfield in the gut. The blow caused the businessman to double over in pain.

"I never said the word 'terrorist!' So, keep that damn word out of your mouth! Do you hear me?"

Mansfield was still doubled over from the blow to his stomach as he coughed and nodded in reply.

Desopo grabbed Mansfield and forced him to stand up straight so that he could look him in the eye. "This is what it comes down to, Mansfield. We need to give our contacts overseas something to appease them. Now, Watkins must have some kind of prototype that we can sell to them."

Mansfield shook his head. "Mr. Watkins works on all his prototypes in his private laboratory. It's at the bottom of the Watkins Building and the only way to access it is from his office."

Desopo pointed to the two men standing behind him. "These two gentlemen are agents Silva and Liddel. They are going to accompany you to the Watkins Building. You are going to take them to this laboratory and show them what prototypes will get us the most money on the black market. Then you are going to bring those prototypes back here to me. Got it?"

All it took was one look at Desopo and his men for Chester Mansfield to realize that this was not a request he could say no to. He nodded and then followed the two men back to the limousine.

Mansfield climbed into the back of the limousine and looked at the two deadly CIA agents sitting on either side of him. The small man shook his head in disbelief.

"My god, what have I gotten myself into?" he muttered to himself. "I just wanted to improve the value of the company and make some extra money on the side. Now I'm breaking into my boss's office to steal his work and sell it to people of questionable morals."

Agent Silva used his elbow to poke Mansfield in the ribs. "Stop all the whining, will you? We have a job to do and having you cry your eyes out as we walk into the building isn't going to help. You need to look calm and cool to convince the guards to let us into Watkins' office."

The agent then reached into his pocket and pulled out his handgun. "If you aren't able to convince the guard to let us up to the office, then we are going to

58

have to do things the hard way. Trust me, if you think you're in over your head now, this is nothing compared to how over your head you'll be if things get messy in there."

Mansfield was now sweating profusely as he responded. "Okay. I understand. I'll make sure the guard lets us into Watkins' office."

The scared businessman then closed his eyes and began to silently pray that he was able to get these men what they wanted and avoid anyone getting hurt as the car moved ever closer to the Watkins Building.

CHAPTER 9

As the limousine pulled to a stop outside of the Watkins Building, Chester Mansfield took several deep breaths in an attempt to calm himself down before trying to convince the security guards to let him take two complete strangers up to Ben Watkins' office when Watkins wasn't there.

Agent Liddel gestured toward the door and said, "Let's get going, Mansfield. We don't have any time to waste." He then turned on the comm to the driver. "Wait right here. When we come out you take us back to the construction site. Do it quickly but not so quick as to draw unneeded attention to us."

The driver came back with a simple, "Understood."

Mansfield replied, "Okay, okay. Just let me do the talking when we get inside."

The two agents nodded in agreement at Mansfield and then the three men exited the limousine and walked into the front door. Mansfield sighed when he saw the men walking in with two large duffel bags.

He looked at the agents and said, "They are not going to let you in with two bags like that."

"You'd better find out a way to make it happen, Mansfield," Liddel demanded.

Mansfield cringed when he saw the guards at that front desk. He knew them both well. One was Susan Valea; the other was Desean Patterson. They were both parents of multiple children. Mansfield hoped that things went smoothly. He knew these two guards were good, hard working people and he did not want anything to happen to them.

When the three men walked into the door, the guards gave them a suspicious look.

Susan smiled as she walked up to them. "Good evening, Mr. Mansfield. Is there something I can help you with?"

"Yes, so stupid of me," he replied. "I was in Mr. Watkins' office earlier today showing off some prototypes that these men had put together. I foolishly left the prototypes in his office. These gentlemen need those prototypes back so they can make the adjustments Mr. Watkins requested. I've already spoken to Mr. Watkins and he said it would be fine if we could just go up there and grab the stuff I left." Mansfield gestured toward the elevator. "So, if you could just take us up there and unlock the door, we'll get what we need and be on our way."

Susan looked at Desean and said, "I didn't get any call from Mr. Watkins on this. Did you?"

Her fellow guard shook his head. "No," he responded, "but a quick phone call to Mr. Watkins can clear this whole thing up."

Desean was in the middle of dialing his employer when agent Silva pointed a gun at him. "Put the phone down."

Desean complied but kept the phone call active.

***

Raptor had decided that a discreet entrance into his office from his laboratory would be faster than changing back to Ben Watkins, going up to office with his Raptor gear hidden, then changing back to the hero. Hence, his chosen M.O. was to swing across the street and grab the scales from the statue of Lady Justice. He was in his elevator, when his visor alerted him that he had an incoming call from the security desk at the front of the building.

Raptor switched on the phone call and turned off his voice modulator, so he sounded like Ben Watkins and not his alter-ego.

"Hey, Desean. What is up?"

Rather than a reply from the security guard. He heard agent Liddel telling Desean to put the phone down.

Raptor immediately increased the volume on his visor so he could hear what the people on the other side of the phone were saying to his security staff as his elevator continued to make its way to Ben Watkins' office.

Liddel continued to yell commands at Susan and Desean. "Back away from the desk! Then slowly take out the keys to open Watkins' door and toss them over to us!"

Desean did as the agent said and took the requested items out of his pocket and tossed them to Liddel. As he did so he queried in a louder than normal voice to make sure the phone picked up what he was saying, "Mr. Mansfield, why are you working with these men to break into Mr. Watkins office?"

Mansfield's eyes went wide when he heard Desean say his name. "He's still got the call to Watkins open! He knows that we are here!"

Liddel and Silva opened fire on the two security guards. Both Susan and Desean dropped behind the security desk. Susan pressed a panic button that not only alerted the Port City police, but also activated a bullet proof shield to rise out of the ground and surround the security desk. The two security guards kept their heads low as the bullets bounced off the shield and fell to the ground.

Mansfield looked at the agents and shouted. "Watkins has probably already called the police! We need to get up to his office, get into his lab, grab what we can, and then get the hell out of here!" The agents ran over to the elevator and took it up to the top floor and Ben Watkins' office.

While they were ascending, Mansfield began shaking and screaming, "My life is over! My life is over! Watkins knows I was here trying to get into his office! The security guards know too!" He threw his hands in the air. "For Christ's sakes, I'm on camera with you two as you tried to shoot up the place!"

Silva grabbed Mansfield and slammed him against the wall. "Shut up, Mansfield!" the agent yelled. "How did you think this was going to end once the deal fell through?" He took his hand off the businessman. "Don't worry, Desopo will take care of you. He always planned to. You'll be fine when this is all said and done. Right now, you need to calm down and help us get what we can from Watkins and salvage something from this whole situation."

Mansfield nodded in acquiescence. "Okay. I can do this. We can still make this work." He looked at Silva and said, "What does Desopo have planned for me?"

Silva growled, "Not now, Mansfield. Keep your mind on the mission."

As the three men made their way up to the top of the building, Raptor stepped out of the elevator from his laboratory and into his office. He climbed out of his window and onto the ledge outside of his office. Then he waited for the assailants. They would be expecting to find an empty office but instead they would find Raptor swinging in through the window to engage them.

When the elevator opened, Mansfield, Silva, and Liddel sprinted over to Watkins' office. Mansfield rushed over to the door and used the keys security had given him to open it. Once the entrance to the office was opened, he ran to the back wall where Watkins' elevator was. The two agents quickly entered the office behind Mansfield.

They were halfway across the room when Raptor leaped in through the window, slammed into Liddel, and sent him crashing into Silva. All three men went to the floor in a jumbled heap. Silva's gun flew out of his hands as he tumbled across the carpet.

Liddel and Raptor both immediately sprang to their feet. The agent tried to point his gun at Raptor, but the crime fighter quickly struck the firearm and sent it flying across the room.

As Liddel and the vigilante were squaring off Mansfield took one look at the hero and screamed, "Raptor is here? Hell no! I'm out!"

He then ran out of the office and hurried down the emergency stairs.

Liddel threw a kick which Raptor blocked with his forearm. The hero then stepped forward and hit the agent with a jab to the face. Liddel stumbled backward as Silva stood up and punched Raptor in the face. The blow snapped the hero's head back, but his visor and helmet absorbed much of the impact. Raptor pulled his head back to see Silva moving to strike him again as Liddel was standing back up. Silva threw another punch, but Raptor dodged it, grabbed the agent's arm, and then used his own momentum to slam him into the wall.

Liddel lunged forward and wrapped his arms around Raptor. The agent squeezed as hard as he could and screamed to his partner, "I've got him! Get your gun and shoot him!"

Silva went to grab his piece when Raptor threw his head back and smashed his helmet into Liddel's nose, shattering it on impact. He then turned around and hit the bleeding agent in the face, knocking him down, while simultaneously grabbing one of the spheres from his bandoliers and ducking.

Raptor was crouched down as he turned around and saw Silva firing a volley of bullets over his head. The vigilante hurled the sphere in his hand at Silva. When the object hit the agent, it exploded in a cloud of tear gas. Silva was choking on the gas while Raptor's visor filtered out the debilitating substance.

Raptor moved through the white cloud that was filling his office when Liddel got back to his feet and tackled the vigilante from behind. The CIA agent tried to use his weight to pin the crime fighter to the ground but with the latter's own considerable strength enhanced by the exo-suit Raptor was able to stand up even with Liddel on top of him. The hero pulled the agent off his back, lifted him over his head, and slammed him into the floor. Liddel gasped as the impact knocked the air out of his lungs. He then inhaled a mouthful of tear gas which set him into a brief coughing fit before causing the agent to pass out.

Raptor turned to see Silva stumbling toward him through the cloud of tear gas. The agent threw a weak punch at Raptor. The crime fighter easily dodged the blow and delivered a snap kick to Silva's head that rendered him unconscious.

The vigilante then secured the two assailants and moved out of the window. Once he was outside, he saw police cars moving toward the Watkins Building. Raptor was both angry and disappointed at Chester Mansfield for his betrayal. Despite his feelings, he knew that he could track down Mansfield later. Right now, his focus had to be on stopping Retribution.

Raptor aimed his gauntlets at the top of the courthouse across the street and fired a baton with a repelling cord attached to it at the statue. The rod wrapped around the body of the statue and when the crime fighter knew it was secure, he swung out across the street.

Raptor landed on the roof next to the statue. He looked at the large figurine as he was taking the scales out of its hands and said, "I'm just borrowing this. I promise I'll return it as soon as I'm done with it."

Raptor attached the scales to his bandoliers and swung back across the street to his office. When the hero entered the room, he saw the elevator making its way back up to his floor. The hero had no doubt the conveyance was full of police. Raptor quickly dashed across the room and ran to his elevator.

He took it down to his private lab and gave a command to his visor, "Show the security feed from Ben Watkins' office". As Raptor exited his private lab and entered the transport that would take him back to his lair, he saw the police arresting the agents he had just fought.

The hero walked on to the subterranean monorail as he gave another command into his visor: "Bring up a list of recently missing college students from Port City University."

A list of three students came up, and the name of a basketball player, Charles Donnor, immediately stood out to the vigilante. As he investigated Coach Flanagan's death Raptor began to suspect that the coach and several of his players may have been involved in a point shaving scheme.

He commanded, "Show me the statistics for Charles Donnor, single out games when Port City University was unable to cover a point spread."

Raptor's visor displayed Donnor's statistics, which confirmed his suspicion that the athlete was taking part in the point shaving scheme. The player's size and weight were also a match for the revenant Raptor had seen on the security video heading toward Flanagan's office.

Raptor now knew where he had to look to determine who Donnor's next victim would be. He spoke into his visor, "Show me a list of known bookies and loan sharks who've bet on Port City University's point spread."

The supercomputer that was attached to Raptor's visor started working on hacking dozens of gambling websites and bank accounts. The AI took several minutes to acquire the requested information. When it had finally collated all the information a list of five names appeared.

Raptor looked at the list and mentally compared it to the stats of Charles Donnor's final game. Realizing that the Donnor had played exceedingly well in his last game he deduced that at least one of these bookies had lost big on it.

The AI once more completed its search and showed the names of Barney "The Barracuda" Cheaney and his enforcer Mike "The Moose" McConnel.

Raptor's transport came to a stop in his lair as he looked at the two names. The hero said to himself, "Moose is the muscle of the organization. He did the dirty work. He's likely the next target."

Raptor placed the scales he had taken from the statue of justice in a safe that was embedded in the floor of his sanctuary. He then jumped onto his motorcycle and drove out to the last known address of Moose McConnel.

***

Chester Mansfield was hyperventilating as the limousine made its way back toward the construction site and Agent Desopo.

Mansfield's mind was swirling with thoughts about what had just occurred. He knew that his life as he knew it was over. He was for sure going to lose his job and would likely face criminal charges. Even if he went on the run, Raptor had seen him there. The vigilante was well known for tracking down any person who was in his crosshairs.

Mansfield started talking to himself out loud as the driver took him back to the construction site. "Desopo works for the CIA. If anyone can hide me where Raptor will never find me, it's the CIA."

Mansfield realized that he was nearly drenched in sweat from all the stress he was under. He took off his coat and threw it over his shoulder as the limo came to a stop at the construction site. Mansfield took a deep breath and then started walking over toward Desopo. Standing beside him was the remaining agent of his team and a blonde woman in tight fitting leather clothes with a long black coat, and what looked like a sword hanging from a hilt around her waist. Mansfield had no idea who the woman was, but he had a hard time taking his eyes off her. The executive felt as if she were somehow drawing him to the vixen.

Desopo gave a suspicious look at Mansfield when he saw him coming back alone. "Where in the hell are Silva and Liddel? And where are the prototypes you were supposed to bring back?"

Mansfield frowned and replied, "Your men opened fire on the security guards, forcing them to activate a bullet proof barrier. Then when we tried to make it into Watkins' office, Raptor was there waiting for us."

Desopo threw his hands up in frustration while exclaiming, "Raptor is mixed up in this now? Jesus Christ did you screw things up, Mansfield! Where are Silva and Liddel now?"

"I barely escaped Raptor myself. I guess he took them down. As we were driving away, I saw several police cars heading toward the building. They are probably in police custody by now."

"Goddamn it!" Desopo cursed. "The freaking cops got them?" He looked back toward the other agent and the girl. "McKinney, we need to take care of this."

The agent nodded and walked to a nearby cement mixing truck. He climbed into the vehicle and turned it on. The girl just continued to stare intensely at Mansfield, and her glare was both hypnotic and terrifying at the same time. Mansfield felt that she was simultaneously looking into his soul and somehow putting him under her thrall.

Desopo walked over and grabbed Mansfield by his soaking wet shirt. "You just ran away didn't you, Mansfield? You just ran away and left my men to fight Raptor and the police!"

As Desopo was yelling at the businessman, Agent McKinney backed the vehicle up to a large pit that had been dug for a foundation to be poured. He then pulled the lever to let the concrete start filling the quarry.

"Raptor was tearing your men apart!" Mansfield pleaded. "What did you want me to do? Get caught by the police too?"

Desopo shook his head. "Not getting caught by the cops was the only thing you've gotten right in this whole damned situation!" spat the CIA man.

Mansfield did his best to calm down as he looked Desopo in the eye. "I've got Raptor and now the police after me. Silva said you were going to take care of me. So, what's the plan? How are you going to take care of me?"

Desopo shook his head. "How dense are you, Mansfield? Don't you know what 'take care of' means in CIA talk?" Desopo pulled Mansfield to the pit where the agent was pouring the cement, and he tossed the hapless businessman into it.

Mansfield fell face first into the wet concrete. He immediately pulled himself up and looked at Desopo, McKinney, and the woman – all of whom were standing at the edge of the pit looking down at him as the concrete rose past his knees.

The doomed executive began to panic as he yelled to Desopo, "Wait! You can't do this! I won't talk! I can still be helpful to you! I -I still have friends at Watkins' company. I can reach out to them to get you those prototypes."

Desopo shook his head and replied, "After the fiasco today, there is no way we are ever going to be able to get back inside the Watkins Building. At this point, all I can do is minimize the damage. That starts with tying up as many loose ends as possible."

Mansfield screamed as the concrete passed his waist. "No! You can't do this to me! I tried my best! I tried my best!"

"It's over for you, Mansfield," was Desopo's response. "At least die with your dignity intact. Stop screaming like a child and just accept it."

Mansfield looked at the agent and saw that there was no sympathy in his eyes. He then shifted his gaze to the girl who was still looking at him as if he were the only thing in the world right now. He felt more drawn to the mysterious woman than he had ever before.

"Please," the businessman began pleading to her. "Please help me."

Retribution floated down from the edge of the pit. Her body seemed to slide into the cement without being affected by it. It was almost as if the quickly hardening liquid was passing right through her. Mansfield had enough presence of mind to take a quick look at Desopo and McKinney to see that they were totally unaffected by what Retribution was doing. It was almost as if they did not see her.

The viscous liquid had reached Mansfield's shoulder when he looked into Retribution's piercing blue eyes. "Help me," he whimpered.

The goddess smiled at him and replied in her ghostly voice, "I can't help you yet, but when this is all over I will. And trust me, what we do next will be so much more fun with you encased in concrete."

The goddess of vengeance then kissed him. She pulled her lips away as the cement reached Mansfield's chin. She waved at him as she levitated out of the concrete without a drop of the chalky substance on her.

Retribution waved at Mansfield as she ascended out of the pit. "Goodbye, Chester," she said softly. "I have another of my clients to see right now. I shall be back for you tomorrow after you dry out. Before I go, I can give you one bit of good news, however. Two of the four people you want revenge on are the same person." She winked. "Where do you think Raptor gets all of that hi-tech crime fighting gear from and why do you think he was in Ben Watkins' office?"

Mansfield watched Retribution fly away into the night sky. Then as the liquified concrete started to seep into his mouth and up to his eyes he looked at Desopo and McKinney. As the cement reached his eyes, Mansfield held his gaze on the two CIA agents with nothing on his mind but exacting revenge on those who had killed him.

As the concrete covered his head and he found himself in complete darkness Chester Mansfield had the names of four men in his mind who needed to exact his revenge on: Desopo, his subordinate agent McKinney, and Raptor/Ben Watkins

CHAPTER 10

Moose McConnel was sitting on his sofa and watching baseball. The Barracuda did not need him to work tonight and he had used some of his money to pick up a girl earlier in the day. After paying the woman for her services and sending the hooker on her way, he had the rest of the night to relax.

The hitman had just opened his third beer and sat down on his coach when, outside of his house, the storm drain at the end of the street popped out of its moorings. The hulking form of the undead Charles Donner crawled out of the sewer system and moaned in anger. The bag-headed horror was still carrying the axe he had taken from the university as he looked around and saw Retribution floating in the street next to him.

The goddess pointed down the street and said, "Three houses down on the right. The 'Moose' is waiting there for you." She gestured toward the axe and smiled. "With a name like Moose do you think his head would look nice mounted on a wall if you were to lop it off?"

Charles' only response was to grunt. The revenant then adjusted the potato sack over his head so that he could see out of it and began walking toward Moose's house. The giant moved with a slow and lumbering walk. With each step he took, Charles left a trail of salt water and seaweed as the two substances oozed out of his putrid skin and dropped to the ground behind him.

When he reached Moose's house he started walking toward the door. He was going to smash through it when Retribution stopped him.

The goddess pointed at the power box outside of Moose's house. "Did you die a quick painless death, or did you die slowly in utter terror surrounded by darkness?"

The revenant once more grunted in reply. He then lumbered over to the power box, grabbed it in his powerful hands, and yanked it out of the wall. Sparks flew into the air, silhouetting the revenant in a bright flash before turning the entire house dark. Charles dropped the still sparking wires and then walked around to the back of the residence.

Inside his abode, Moose was startled by the loss of power. "What the fu--" the hitman began to say before his sentence was cut short by a fire axe smashing through his back door.

Moose quickly grabbed his gun from the table next to him and ran into the kitchen. He watched as the axe was pulled out of his back door and slammed into it a second time. Moose was trying to see who was axing his way into his house when a powerful kick shattered the entrance to splinters and sent the wooden debris flying into the kitchen. The hitman's body shook with fear when he saw the still dripping wet form of Charles Donnor standing at his door with an axe in his hand.

"You- you're supposed to be dead," Moose stammered while shaking his head.

Charles started moving toward the hitman as the latter emptied the clip of his colt .45 into the revenant's body. The bullets failed to even slow the undead creature down. Charles walked through Moose's barrage, lifted his axe over his head, and then used it to slice the burly man's right hand off. Blood sprayed over both Moose and Charles as the hitman's gun dropped to the floor along with a large portion of his hand.

The injured man dropped to his knees shouting in agony as blood continued spewing from the remnants of his severed metacarpus. Charles lifted his axe over his head to finish off the killer who had chained him and tossed him the bay to drown when Retribution called out to him.

"Do not finish him off yet! Savor your vengeance, as with the coach! Make him feel the pain and suffering that you felt!" She floated over to the undead horror. "He is the one who placed that bag over your head. Don't you think it's time he wore it?"

Charles dropped his axe on the floor. He then reached up and pulled the potato sack off his head. Moose screamed again – this time in horror – when he saw the dead man's' gray, waterlogged, and decaying face. He stood up to run away when the revenant grabbed the hitman and slammed him to the floor. The walking abomination stood above his victim and mumbled something incoherent that caused more salt water and bit of seaweed to drip out of his mouth and onto Moose's face.

Charles placed one powerful hand around the man's neck and then pulled the potato sack over Moose's head. The mob enforcer was nearly gagged by the combined smell of the bay at low tide and a rotting corpse that permeated the interior of the satchel.

With the paid killer now completely at his mercy, Charles looked to Retribution as to what to do next.

The goddess smiled as she gestured to the stove. "He killed you by water," she said. "It would only be fitting if you killed him by fire." The divine being heard the sound of a motorcycle behind her and sighed. "Him again? Well, I'll be taking care of him soon enough."

Raptor was speeding toward Moose McConnel's house when he saw a trail of seaweed on the ground. Knowing that he was already too late, he pushed his motorcycle to the limit. As the assassin's 's house came into view, Raptor noticed a large bay window next to the front door. The hero aimed his motorcycle at the glass pane and then pulled up when he hit the curb. The move sent his bike flying into the air and through the window.

Glass exploded into the Moose's living room as Raptor leaped off his cycle and let it slam into the wall.

"Let go of him!" the crime fighter shouted as he ran toward the undead form of Charles.

The undead monster did not respond. He simply continued to stare at Raptor as if he could not figure out what to do with the vigilante. Raptor made the monster's choice easy for him by punching the revenant in the face. The hero moved like lightning as he followed the punch to the face with two roundhouse punches to the ribs and a looping kick to the back of Charles' head; all of which had no effect on the creature.

With a single back hand Charles sent Raptor flying across the room. The hero's back smashed into the wall and nearly through it. The vigilante was pulling his body out of the crumbled stucco when Retribution appeared next to him.

"There is nothing you can do to stop him," she boasted. "I told you the last time that you would not be able to convince another of my clients to forego their revenge."

Raptor ignored the goddess and kept his focus on Charles as he dragged the screaming Moose toward the stove. The crime fighter sprinted across the room and sprang into the air. He then brought his hand down in a knife edge strike with enough force to shatter a cinder block onto the hand Charles was using to hold onto Moose. As before, the vigilante's blow had no effect on the revenant. Raptor followed the knife edge strike with an elbow to Charles' face.

The monster once more tried to back hand the crime fighter, but this time Raptor was ready for the attack and he ducked it. The hero connected with an uppercut to the monster's chin and then two more hooks to Charles' ribs.

Raptor struck the creature with more than enough force to splinter bones but no matter what he did the reanimated corpse was unfazed by his blows. Charles attempted to backhand the crime fighter a third time, but again the hero was able to duck the blow and hit the dead man two more times in the face. The revenant growled in frustration, let go of Moose, and used both hands to grab Raptor by the shoulders.

"Moose, run!" the hero yelled as he was lifted into the air.

The hitman stood up and sprinted toward his front door. Charles roared in anger, he then turned and threw Raptor through the back wall of the kitchen and into the backyard. The revenant then picked his axe up off the floor and hurled it at the fleeing killer. The weapon buried itself in Moose's lower back, severing his spine and causing him to stumble to the floor.

Charles was moving toward Moose when Retribution spoke into his ear, "He's not going anywhere. You are going to have to make sure the hero cannot keep interfering in your revenge if you hope to carry it out in a satisfying manner."

In the backyard, Raptor rolled over and groaned. He had gotten himself to a sitting position when Charles lumbered out of the shattered back door and started walking toward him. The hero grabbed one of the spheres from his bandoliers and tossed it at the approaching revenant. The sphere exploded on Charles and covered him in liquid nitrogen. The monster managed to take two more steps before being frozen in place. Raptor took a deep breath and then saw Retribution standing next to him.

The goddess was giving the visored hero an annoyed look. "Do you really think that freezing him will stop us?"

"I've hit him enough times to know that, unlike you, he is completely corporeal," The vigilante retorted.

Retribution smiled. "That is not what I asked. I asked if you thought that freezing him would stop us. Because it won't."

She waved her hand in Charles' direction and the ice that had been coating the revenant's body melted away.

Charles shook his body and then roared at Raptor. The hero aimed his gauntlet at the defrosted undead man and fired a baton at him. Thousands of volts of electricity danced over the monster's body when the airborne truncheon struck Charles, but it did nothing to slow his progress.

Raptor quickly grabbed an incendiary sphere and threw it at the advancing entity. The revenant's body burst into flames, but he ignored the fire and simply kept coming for the caped crusader. The blaze enveloping Charles was dying off from the salt water that seeped out of his body when he reached the vigilante. Raptor tried in vain one more time to strike the undead man in the face, but the blow failed to even change the direction Charles' head was facing. The monstrous corpse grabbed Raptor by the neck and slammed into the ground several times.

When Charles finally stopped smashing his adversary into the pavement the hero was barely conscious. There was nothing he could do as the revenant dragged the vigilante over to the chain link fence that surrounded Moose's yard. Charles held Raptor in one hand and used the other to rip one end of the mobster's fence out of the ground. He pressed the dazed hero against the metallic hedge and used it to roll the crime fighter up in it.

After only a few seconds, nearly twenty feet of fence were wrapped around Raptor's body. The beaten hero struggled to break free of the metal binds, but it was too much for even his exo-suit to overcome. Charles then dragged the trapped Raptor onto the porch outside the backdoor. He placed him there and then walked back into the house.

Raptor saw Retribution floating in the air next to him. "Why did he drag me here?" the hero queried.

The mythical creature gestured toward the shattered kitchen door. "So that you can see your efforts were in vain," she replied. "And so, you know what happens to those whom my revenants desire revenge on."

Raptor looked back into the house to see Charles pull the crying form of Moose McConnel over toward the stove. The monster turned the stove on and placed the hitman's right hand into the flame. Raptor watched helplessly as Moose screamed in pain while his remaining hand was burned to the bone.

73

Once he was done with that, Charles did the same thing to what little remained of Moose's other hand.

There was nothing Raptor could do but watch as the process was repeated to every inch of Moose's torso. The man went from screaming to crying to simply moaning as his body was burned away piece by piece. When Charles finally got to Moose's face, he turned the hitman's head so that he was looking out the door and at Raptor. The bound vigilante could almost see a look of relief on Moose's face as Charles took the potato sack off his victim's head and pushed it into the flames. Raptor had to turn away when the contract killer's 's eyes burst from the heat pouring into them. The blind and crippled hitman screamed one final time before he died.

When the prolonged murder was finally over Raptor turned his head toward Retribution. "Moose was a criminal and murderer," the hero stated, "and he deserved to go to jail for his crimes. But he didn't deserve to be tortured like that."

Retribution landed on the ground and put her face in front of Raptor's before responding. "So, he should have faced the justice and punishment of you and the people of this city? Or was it better that the person he killed, the person he drowned, the person he murdered, decide how to punish him? Is it better that the people of the city prescribe what they feel is the proper consequence, or that the victim inflicts what he feels is the deserved punishment?"

Charles was walking toward Raptor with his potato sack in one hand and his axe in the other as the vigilante replied, "Not acting in the same manner as a criminal would when deciding on punishments is what makes a just and civilized society. The people of the city act with more humanity and compassion than the criminals do. That's what makes them functional members of society and not criminals themselves." He looked at Charles as the undead horror pulled his potato sack back over his head. "Unlike the murderous abomination you turned a college student into."

Retribution addressed Charles as he walked over to her. "Loosen him enough that he can free himself when we are gone. I do not want the police to find him here. You and I have one more stop to make before revenge comes looking for Raptor and for Ben Watkins."

Charles tore half of the fence that was wrapped around Raptor off his body. He then started walking back toward the storm drain with Retribution floating beside him.

As they were walking away, and Raptor was freeing himself from the remainder of the metal encumberment, he called out to them.

"I'll see you both tomorrow night at the Barracuda's house!"

Retribution looked back over her shoulder. "After you watch us kill him," she said, I will see you a few days from now back in your lair… where you will finally suffer my wrath."

Raptor had almost pulled himself out of the fence as he whispered, "Maybe I won't be the only thing you see there."

CHAPTER 11

Ben Watkins awoke on Monday morning and his entire body ached. Even with the protection offered by his exo-suit the beating that the reanimated Charles Donnor had put on him had been extensive. His body was covered in bruises and the suit he wore last night had been damaged beyond repair. He had other suits that he could use, but his body would need at least a few days before he was fully healed.

Aside from the pain, he had not slept well after watching the horrific manner in which Moose McConnel was tortured. He was also coming to grips with the fact that he was physically unable to stop Retribution or her revenants. His only option appeared to be trying to contact Nemesis and then, if he was even able to summon her, convince the goddess of vengeance that what her assistant was doing was *not just punishment.*

Even if he was able to work out all those steps this entire plan was based on myth. There was no evidence that Nemesis even believed in *just punishment.* Nemesis was the goddess of vengeance, it was entirely possible that she was only concerned with vengeance, and that justice as a concept with no meaning to her.

The other thing that had kept him awake was the break in at his office and the betrayal of Chester Mansfield. After his run-in with Charles and Retribution, he had received numerous calls from his office and the police. This forced him to return home after his battle, change back into Ben Watkins, then to visit his office where the police were waiting for him. While he had already seen many strange things that day, even he was unprepared for the information he received when he reached the Watkins Building.

The police detective on site had informed him that his office had been broken into by three men, one of whom was his employee and a member of his executive team. The three men battled with the vigilante known as Raptor. The crime fighter had managed to capture two of the men while Mansfield escaped. Ben was already aware of all of this. What he was not aware of was that the two men he had captured appeared on no known database. Despite this fact, they were taken into federal custody almost as soon as they reached the police station.

This information combined with the fighting techniques that he had seen them utilize as Raptor suggested to him that the two men were government operatives, likely Central Intelligence Agency. The CIA had been trying to obtain contracts with his company for years. That would also explain how Chester Mansfield had seemingly managed to disappear. Ben was well aware that the CIA were experts at hiding people or disposing of them.

The police explained that they felt the break in was likely an attempt at corporate espionage. Chester Mansfield would have been one of the people who knew that Ben's private laboratory was behind his office. They also suggested that after Ben had turned down Mansfield's bids for military contracts that he tried to steal some prototypes to sell to a rival company. The police assured Ben that they would continue looking for Mansfield, find out who was behind the burglary attempt, and that they would follow up with the feds on the two men who were taken into custody.

Ben knew that this was just their attempt to placate him. He was reasonably sure that the police knew there was some government angle to this that was over their heads. They were likely thankful that Raptor intervened and prevented anything from being stolen, thus making their job much easier. Ben thanked the police for their help and made a mental note to find Chester Mansfield or more likely at least what was left of him. From there he would decide how to approach the situation with the CIA.

Once his work with the police was done, Ben was finally able to head home at around 3:00 am. It was one of the many instances where he was glad he owned his company so that he could literally show up to work at any time he felt like.

Ben was heading toward the shower when a calendar reminder went off on his phone. He quickly checked his reminders to see that he was supposed to be at the American History Museum in two hours to open the Ulysses S. Grant attraction that his company was supporting. He also had an email that indicated someone had broken into one of the construction sites he was funding. It seemed that an unknown individual had poured concrete into what was supposed to be the foundation of the new building. The strange thing was that it also looked like after the concrete had dried, they dug out a huge hole in the center of the foundation. From what the email indicated, the hole was an easy fix by just pouring concrete into it.

The mystery was the motive for pouring the concrete in the first place and then digging out the center of it. While curious, the matter did not seem to warrant Ben himself addressing the situation. The foreman on site was more than capable of filling out a police report and then refilling the hole in the foundation.

Ben turned on the shower and stepped into the hot water. The spray felt good as the water ran over his battered body. He took a brief moment to simply be human and enjoy the small comfort of a hot shower.

After taking this short relaxation, Ben's thoughts quickly reverted back to the dire situation with Retribution and Charles. The former had confirmed that they would be attacking the Barracuda tonight. She had also said that she would see him in his lair a few days later. It was that declaration that confused Ben. He knew the Barracuda was connected to Charles Donnor's death, but he had no idea how he, as either Raptor or Ben Watkins, was connected to Charles' or anyone else's death.

His primary concern now had to be the Barracuda. His options as to how to save the murderer's life were limited. Warning the mobster as Raptor was an option but what would be the outcome of that action? Even if the Barracuda believed him that a man he had murdered was brought back to life by an ancient goddess as an unstoppable juggernaut, how would he react? A tough guy like the Barracuda was unlikely to run. He was more likely to surround himself with as many of his enforcers as possible. If that occurred, the most probably outcome would be that Charles would simply slaughter everyone between himself and the Barracuda.

As Raptor, Ben had accumulated at least enough evidence to pass onto the police for them to hold the Barracuda for one night. The question then was would Retribution and Charles see a one-night arrest of the Barracuda as apt punishment. At best, that would gain him an extra day before they came for the mobster. In a worst-case scenario, Charles could potentially slash his way through every officer in the precinct to get to the Barracuda. That was not something Ben was going to let happen.

He sat down in the shower as he tried to consider other means by which he could remove the Barracuda from Charles' path. Raptor was running through dozens of scenarios for ways he could try to attack Charles when a thought occurred to him.

He started talking out loud. "Raptor may not be able to save the Barracuda, but perhaps Ben Watkins can."

Watkins jumped out of the shower, quickly dried off, and grabbed his phone. He started getting dressed and made a few calls. The first was to his private pilot, Isabell Mendez.

The phone rang and a feminine but powerful voice answered, "Sparring or flying today?"

"Definitely piloting," Ben replied, "and maybe a little sparring but not with me."

Isabell sighed. "I think I'm going to need a little more clarification on this one."

Ben took a deep breath. "I have something I need you to do, both for me and for my friend."

Isabell knew exactly what Ben meant by "friend." "Okay, what do you both need from me?"

"I need you to fly a couple of people out to Las Vegas for me. I won't be on this trip and these guys… let's just say, they may not be the most reputable company. They will be staying in my hotel out there. I was hoping you could work your way into their group and keep an eye on them for me?" Ben was quiet for a moment. "If this is something, you're uncomfortable with just say the word and I'll think of something else."

Isabell's voice came back almost annoyed. "Have I ever said no to you?" The phone was silent for a minute. "Just answer me this: Will me taking on this mission save lives?"

"Taking these men to Las Vegas will definitely save lives. Keeping an eye on them may also save lives and will almost assuredly prevent several crimes."

Isabell's voice was softer as she said, "If things do get out of hand do you want me to handle it myself or call for help?"

"I'd prefer if you'd call for help. You will be out there as Ben Watkins' pilot. Only resort to handling something yourself if it's a matter of self-defense. That being said, I trust your judgement if you feel you need to intervene in a situation."

"Okay, Ben. I can do this."

"Thank you, Isabell. I owe you."

Isabell laughed. "You can always look to give me a promotion, or at least a pay increase."

"I'm pretty sure we can work out something along those lines. I'll see you at the airport in an hour. Goodbye, Isabell, and be safe on this trip." He then hung up the phone.

Ben's next call was to his personal driver, Eric Perez. Aside from being a driver, his family owned a custom car shop. As such, Eric had a virtual fleet of cars at Ben Watkins' disposal, all with different customizations for various purposes. Once he finished the call with his driver, he phoned one of the hotels he owned in Las Vegas and told them to prepare his penthouse for tonight.

He then quickly got dressed and headed down to meet his driver. As usual, the always punctual Eric was at the curb waiting for him. Eric and Isabell were the only two people who were aware of his double life as both Ben Watkins and Raptor. When he had first started on his path to being a crime fighter, he quickly realized that he needed people he could trust to help him with his cover as Ben Watkins.

He started his search devising an algorithm that would go through military and law enforcement databases for people who met certain criteria. The criteria Ben set were for people who exhibited the utmost loyalty to their position and their team members. The first part of the search was tempered by an additional component that looked for individuals who were willing to voice their opinions when they felt something was wrong or unjust. The search also included parameters for people who were skilled drivers and/or pilots. Lastly, his search parameters included people who had performed acts of unparalleled heroism, such as putting one's own life on the line to save another.

The search yielded several candidates. Ben would interview the contenders as their terms of service came up or when they were due for a promotion. He used his keen detective skills to read the people he interviewed and determine if he felt he could trust them in his crusade against crime.

Eric and Isabell were the only two people who Ben felt he could trust with his secret. After meeting and interviewing them both, offering them substantial pay increases from their previous positions; then, after building up some trust with them, he let them into his world as Raptor.

Eric was a former medical transport driver in the army. He had driven through war zones in Iraq and Afghanistan. As a man who was used to taking on enemy fire and driving through minefields, he was more than qualified enough to drive around Port City. Additionally, he was able to supply medical treatment to Ben in the many instances that he had been injured when fighting crime as Raptor. Eric also had a very dry sense of humor that Ben appreciated. Over time Eric had become not only Ben's driver and trusted ally, but he also became his best friend.

Isabell was a Marine Corps pilot. She had flown in over two dozen fights in her time. Aside from her skills as a pilot, Isabell was one of the most decorated kickboxers in the military. Prior to working for Ben, she had won a silver medal in the last Olympics. Ben often thought that had she had more time to practice the craft in between missions she would have easily won the gold medal. Isabell was so skilled as a hand-to-hand-combatant that Ben often used her as a sparring partner, and she was one of the few fighters he had ever met that could keep up with him.

Aside from her skills as a pilot and kickboxer, Isabell was an extremely interesting, intelligent, and strikingly beautiful woman. Ben often found himself wondering if some day Isabell could be more than just his pilot and sparring partner. For now, the hero decided to keep his potential feelings for her to himself. He felt it would be unfair to Isabell to be both her employer and potential lover. If he was going to take his relationship with Isabell in another direction, he would either have to give up his career as Raptor or find a new pilot, and neither one of those options would be an easy task.

Ben smiled as he walked up to the car and greeted his driver. "Good morning, Eric."

"Good morning, Mr. Watkins," Eric replied with a nod.

Ben slid into the back seat of the car. "Did you stop at the bank, as I asked you to?"

"Of course, sir. The money you requested is in the envelope sitting on the back seat."

"As always, I can certainly count on you, Eric."

"Of course. Where to today, sir?"

"We've got a lot of ground to cover and only a few hours to do it. I need you to take me to 42 Evergreen Lane, then we are going to make a drop-off at the airport, and then back to the American History Museum by 10:00 am. Do you think you can pull that off?"

Eric looked into the rearview mirror so he could see his employer. "I believe the saying is, 'buckle up, sir.'"

Fifteen minutes later the limo pulled to a stop at 42 Evergreen Lane, the home of Barney "The Barracuda'" Cheaney.

Eric turned around to look at his employer. "Forgive me, sir, but I am aware of whose house this is. Would you prefer if I approached the individual inside for you?"

Ben shook his head. "Thank you, Eric, but I can handle this situation."

Ben then stepped out of the car and walked up the Barracuda's door. He knocked and it was opened by a burly enforcer he had encountered before as Raptor. Ben did his best to smile at the man as he spoke to him.

"I am here to see Mr. Cheaney."

The guard stared at Ben and replied, "Mr. Cheaney only sees people by appointment."

Ben smiled, "Tell him that Ben Watkins is here to see him and that I have one thousand dollars for ten minutes of his time and potentially a lot more to come after that."

The guard nodded. "Wait here. I'll see if Mr. Cheaney is free." He then closed the door and left Ben waiting on the porch.

Less than a minute later, the guard returned. "Mr. Watkins, Mr. Cheaney will see you now."

The guard motioned for Ben to follow him and then he led him to the Barracuda's office. The large man knocked on the door and when a voice said, "Come in," the guard opened it and gestured for Ben to enter the office. As Ben walked in the guard closed the door behind him.

The thin rat-like man known as the Barracuda stood and gave Ben a strange look as he walked into his office. "What does billionaire Ben Watkins want with a humble man like me?"

"I'm told that you are the man to see about sports betting in this area" Ben answered with a smile.

"That's true and I am always looking to take on new clients. Especially ones of your status." He gestured for Ben to sit down. "What kind of action are you looking for? Baseball, hoops, hockey, boxing, college sports?"

Ben was scanning the room as soon as he walked into it. He took notice of a large picture behind the Barracuda's desk and identified it as a likely cover for a safe.

In response to the bookie's question, Ben smiled again at the mobster and shook his head. "Mr. Cheaney, I'm not much of a gambler. I'm more of an investor. I'm told that you might have some potential investment opportunities for me."

The Barracuda shook his head. "I'm sorry, Mr. Watkins, but I don't think…"

The businessman cut off the mobster before he could continue. "Please let me finish."

He reached into his pocket and took out the envelope with the money he had asked Eric to retrieve for him. He handed it over to the Barracuda.

"Here's the grand I mentioned just for your time right now," Ben continued. "I'm fully aware that there may be people listening to us here that could make it difficult to talk business. To show you I am serious about my willingness to invest in new endeavors, I was hoping that I could treat you and several of your men to a few days at my hotel in Las Vegas. You can fly out on my personal plane, all of your expenses will be covered by me, you can stay in my penthouse, and additionally I will give you another forty-nine grand just to come out this weekend with me."

He could see that he now had the bookie's attention. He continued, "And that's just a taste of what is waiting for you if I can invest in your operations."

The Barracuda's face lit up at the extravagant offer. "Fifty grand and a full expense paid week in Vegas just to hear you out?"

Ben nodded in affirmation. "The only condition is that you have to leave now. I will send you out in my plane. I will take care of a few appointments I have here, and then meet you out in Vegas in two days. I can assure you that my penthouse is secure. We can discuss business there without any concern of third parties listening in. So, what do you say, Mr. Cheaney? Is my offer worth you at least hearing me out?"

The Barracuda nodded. "Give me and my men ten minutes, and we will meet you at your car."

Ben stood up and shook the Barracuda's hand. "I look forward to doing business with you, Mr. Cheaney."

***

An hour later, the Barracuda and two of his bodyguards were on Ben's plane as it was preparing for flight. Isabell looked down from the cockpit and gave her boss a wink and smile before taking off. These gestures were the pilot's way of indicating she was prepared for the mission her employer had given to her.

Ben smiled back at her and with that, the Barracuda and his crew were on their way to Las Vegas. As per Ben's instructions, Isabell would keep an eye on the Barracuda and his men while they were there. As an attractive and engaging female, she would not have an issue convincing the Barracuda to let her party with him and his crew.

As the flight took off, Eric asked Ben, "Did you accomplish what you had hoped for, boss?"

"At least a short-term goal," he replied, "and if things work out as I hope they do, putting that man on a plane may help me kill two birds with one stone."

"Given that you want Isabell to stay close to those – I shudder to use the term 'men – do you think they'll behave themselves around her?"

Ben laughed. "If they try anything that Isabell is uncomfortable with, she'll make whatever Retribution and Charles have planned for them seem like a day at the spa in comparison."

"I'm inclined to agree with you, sir."

Ben checked his watch. "Can you still get me to the museum in an hour?"

Eric nodded. 'Without question, sir." The two men then started walking back to the limo.

Forty-five minutes later, Ben Watkins was standing in the museum at the entrance to the Ulysses S. Grant exhibit. The display was blocked off by a ribbon and a crowd was anxiously waiting for Ben to give a speech and then open the exhibit.

Ben looked at the people standing before him and it made his heart leap with joy. As much good as he did fighting crime as Raptor, he felt as if the real difference he made in the city came from the social programs he helped to fund. Helping to bring special exhibits to the museum was just one of the ways in

84

which he tried to enrich his community and inspire the next generation to rise above the temptation of living a life of crime.

For moments like this, Ben never wrote up a speech ahead of time. Rather, he tried to let the people of his city inspire him just as he hoped that his actions inspired them. He focused on the group of school children whom the Watkins Charity had paid for to come see the exhibit. He smiled when he saw their beaming faces because they helped to bring the words, he needed to him.

Ben took a deep breath and then began his speech. "Thank you all for coming. Like many of you I am a lover of history and the great men and women who helped to shape our world. Today we open an exhibit on Ulysses S. Grant.

"Grant was a flawed man who lived in a difficult time. Despite his faults and living through one of the darkest periods in our country's history, he did his best to rise to the challenge when he was called upon. Grant led the Union forces against his country's own soldiers. He did this because he was called upon to do so and because he knew he was fighting for a greater good."

Ben took another deep breath before continuing with his speech.

"I brought this exhibit here because I thought we could all learn from it. There are many evils which take place in our city on a daily basis. Sometimes we see them occur and do nothing about it. Sometimes we are asked by our friends or our family to take place in those evils. It could not have been easy for Grant to challenge his own country's soldiers, many of whom had previously served under him in other wars.

Still, despite his imperfections, when he was called upon to act for the greater good, he did so. I hope that by walking through this exhibit, by seeing Grant's faults and then by seeing the many things he accomplished despite that, we too can be inspired.

We are all flawed as human beings, but at this moment our city is calling out for us to act. It's calling out for us to call the authorities when we know a crime is going to be committed. It's calling out to us to have the courage to say no if asked to engage in unscrupulous activities by friends and family."

Ben smiled as he paused. "The city is now calling out to me to stop talking so that you can all see this exhibit."

The crowd laughed. Ben then grabbed the giant scissors leaning on the wall next to the exhibit and cut the ribbon across its opening.

He then turned around and said, "Ladies, gentlemen, and children of all ages I now declare this exhibit open!"

The people cheered and followed Ben into the exhibition.

He had only taken a few steps when the curator of the museum walked up next to him and said, "That was an excellent speech, Mr. Watkins. I would like to again thank you for helping to bring this exhibit to our museum."

"Not at all," Ben responded. "It was my pleasure to bring it here."

The curator smiled. "Well, will you at least let me guide you to some of the more interesting pieces in the exhibit?"

Ben nodded and smiled back. "By all means."

The curator led Ben past several interesting documents and photographs. One of the highlights of the exhibit was the sword that Grant wielded when General Robert E. Lee surrendered and ended the Civil War at Appomattox Courthouse. Ben stopped and took a close look at the sword and pointed at the weapon.

"With that sword in hand, Grant officially brought to a close the bloodiest war in our nation's history and ended the evil that was slavery."

"Indeed, he did."

Ben looked at the curator. "Would you say that sword could be looked at as a symbol of justice in our country?"

The steward thought about the question for a minute before responding. "As you said, that sword symbolically ended slavery in our country. I can't think of a more just thing ever done by a sword."

"Me neither."

Ben subsequently walked on to the next exhibit and made a mental note to return to the museum after it had closed as Raptor. Ben intended to borrow the sword of justice just as he had borrowed the scales from the statue of Lady Justice.

CHAPTER 12

Las Vegas

Isabell had just landed her plane and was in the process of docking it. Once the plane was fully docked, she opened the door to the cabin to see the group of criminals that she had just flown to Las Vegas for a few days of fun at Ben Watkins' expense.

When they saw her open the door the men cheered. They were already drunk, having gone through most of the liquor on the plane and their typically disrespectful behavior was even worse than it had been when they had first boarded.

The men stared at Isabell with hungry eyes as they made comments like, "I've got something that needs docking as well." And, "I bet there's more than one landing strip here."

Since she was assigned the task of staying with these men and making sure they did not hurt anyone, the former soldier simply sighed and thought to herself, *What am I doing here, with these idiots?*

She took a deep breath and continued her chain of thoughts. *You're here because you're saving lives. Even if it's the lives of scum like these, you are still saving lives. Remember how many people you killed during your time as a fighter pilot. Now it's time to equal things out by saving some lives. That, and you're madly in love with your boss who happens to be a superhero and out of your reach, but because you want to be around him you do things like this.*

Isabell brushed off the comments of the Barracuda and his men and smiled at them. "I want to have a good time while we're out here, before my boss shows up! Who's with me?"

The men cheered and the Barracuda walked up to Isabell and put his arm around her. "I can show you what it really means to fly, doll."

Isabell gently pulled his hand away from her and replied, "Let's just see how the night goes." She then directed the men off the plane.

An hour later, Isabell had checked into the room next to where the Barracuda and his men were staying. She could handle herself when she needed to but there was no way she was going to stay in a room with a bunch of drunken mobsters.

Isabell put on a dress that did justice to her toned body, looked at herself in the mirror, and said, "All right, girl, you know this is for the greater good. You can do this."

She then walked out into the hallway to find the Barracuda and his men waiting for her. Once more the Barracuda went to put his arm around her, and once more she politely slid away from the man's attempt.

She smiled at them before saying, "I'm in the mood for Blackjack, so who's with me?"

The men cheered once more, and then they headed down into the casino.

Isabell watched the Barracuda and his men as they played at the table. She noticed that for people who were so tied into professional gambling they were terrible at card games. They were losing so badly that she had no concern they were cheating the house. The Barracuda kept ordering drinks for both him and the pilot. Each time the waitress brought Isabella a drink she would politely decline it and ordered water instead.

As he became increasingly intoxicated, the Barracuda would continually ask her why she could not loosen up and have a drink.

Each time he asked, Isabell would remind him that she was a pilot and was on call for her boss. So, while she could have a good time, drinking was not an option.

Once the Barracuda had lost several thousand dollars, he opted to move his crew into the casino's night club.

Isabell was relieved to be able to move around more freely in the club but in the packed establishment, she knew it would be more difficult to keep the Barracuda and his men in her sight.

The Barracuda was nearly on top of her as she made her way onto the dance floor. She moved away from the gangster and started dancing by herself in the middle of the platform. A few men who were not a part of the Barracuda's group and the occasional woman came over to dance with her. Isabell was only looking to enjoy herself, so she danced with all of them. The fact that she was dancing with other people also helped to keep the Barracuda and his men away from her.

After dancing for over an hour, Isabell took a break and made her way over to the bar. She ordered water as one of the Barracuda's men came over and placed his hand on her backside.

The gangster grinned at her as he said, "Come on, pilot. How about you bring me in for a landing like we talked about on the plane?"

Isabell forcefully knocked his hand away from her posterior before replying, "This is one flight that's off limits to you."

The man reached out for her again. "Come on, babe. You know what they say about Vegas and what happens here."

The pilot pushed his arm away a second time. "Trust me, if you touch me again your broken finger will follow you back to Port City."

The gangster shrugged. "Whatever. There's plenty of other bitches here."

As the man was walking away the Barracuda came up behind Isabell. "He can be such an asshole. He has no idea how to treat a lady." He then gestured to the dance floor. "Would you care to dance?"

Inwardly, the rat-like gangster made her skin crawl, but she had to admit dancing with him was the easiest way to make sure he stayed out of trouble. She took to the floor and was at least pleased that one of her favorite songs was playing. She tried to lose herself in the song and forget who she was dancing with. As she was bopping with the Barracuda, she kept shifting her body and her eyes so that she could see the rest of his crew.

One man was dancing with another woman, while the man who had just attempted to feel her up was sitting at the bar having a drink. Another song came on and she stayed on the dance floor with the Barracuda as she continued to watch his two bodyguards. The man at the bar had moved onto harassing another woman who also clearly did not care for his hands-on approach.

After a few more minutes of dancing, Isabell turned her head back toward the bodyguard at the bar to see another man standing between him and the woman he had been making advances toward. It seemed the man was trying to

89

tell the bodyguard to back down after the woman had asked him to do so several times.

Their heated conversation hit a breaking point when the bodyguard threw a drink in the man's face and pushed him. Isabell saw the guard reaching into his coat pocket and she darted across the club to the bar.

As the bodyguard was taking out his knife, Isabell grabbed the hand with the blade and said, "Put the knife down or I will break your hand." She glared at him when he failed to immediately respond. "You are out here representing Mr. Watkins as part of a business deal. I can guarantee you if you try to stab someone in his club any chance your boss had of doing business with Mr. Watkins will be gone."

The bodyguard angrily replied, "Get your hand off me, bitch."

He then threw a punch which Isabell ducked. She then stood up and struck the man with the palm of her hand in his nose, breaking it. At the same time, she twisted the man's hand with the knife in it, breaking several of his fingers.

The man fell to the floor wracked in pain as a crowd of people gathered around them.

The Barracuda went over to his man and grabbed him by the shirt. "You dumbass," he said, "if your short temper screwed this deal up for us, I swear I will gut you like a fish."

He then turned around to Isabell. "I'm incredibly sorry for my associate's conduct," he lamented. "My main bodyguard Moose failed to answer his phone this morning. So, I had to take this clown instead. Please inform your boss that he will be reprimanded by me for his actions."

A large security guard walked over to where the bodyguard was sitting on the floor, holding his bloody nose and cursing.

The casino employee looked at Isabell and asked, "Is everything good here, Ms. Mendez?"

"Just had to teach this man some manners," the pilot answered with a nod. "He wasn't being very sociable to another lady or her friend." She looked down at the bodyguard she had just injured. "I think an ice pack, a shower, and a good night's sleep will do this man some good." She turned toward the Barracuda, "Maybe if his friends can take him back to his room for the night, I can call Mr. Watkins and let him know that when this man got out of line his employer was quick to address the situation."

"Sure," the Barracuda said. "We can take him back to our room." He smiled. "I think we've all had enough to drink and lost enough money for one night." The gangster laughed as he helped his bodyguard to his feet.

As they walked past the casino security guard, he heard the man cursing about Isabell. He stopped the man and looked him in the eye. "That is one dangerous lady. Be thankful that she went easy on you. I've seen her do a lot worse to guys who really pissed her off."

Isabell watched as the Barracuda and his other bodyguard helped the injured man to his feet and took him to receive medical care.

She apologized to the bartender and security guard, both of whom she was friends with. They both told her not to worry about the situation. Aside from being her friends they knew she was Ben Watkins' personal pilot, meaning that any issue having to do with her had to be reported directly to Watkins himself. Since none of them wanted to tell Watkins what took place, and the police did not become involved in the situation, they saw this little skirmish as a non-issue.

After apologizing to those she felt she needed to, Isabell went up to her room. When she entered the suite, she immediately took off her clothes and jumped into the shower. The pilot stayed under the refreshing spray of water for a long time. She felt as if she needed to use all the water in Las Vegas to wash the slime off her body from being around the Barracuda and his men.

Isabell laid down naked in her bed as she looked at the luxurious suite her boss had provided for her. Once more her mind drifted off to a fantasy where she and Ben Watkins would spend a weekend in Las Vegas in this suite. She replayed the night's events in her head of hitting the card tables with Ben, then dancing in the club, and then… well, whatever would happen when they returned to the room.

As she had a thousand times before, she chided herself for her schoolgirl daydreams. She reminded herself that Ben was her boss, and that as far as she could tell, Raptor would always be his first and only love.

Her mind was brought back to the present when she heard a knock on her door and the Barracuda's voice on the other side of it. "Hey, babe. It's me. I left those losers next door. Why don't you let me in, and we can kiss and make up?"

Isabell just sat silently in her bed as the advances of the Barracuda drove any remaining thoughts of Ben Watkins from her mind.

The Barracuda knocked again. "Babe, are you awake?"

Isabell walked over to her door and said, "I just got off the phone with Mr. Watkins. He suggests that after the events involving your friend, we should all turn in for the night. If you want to keep this potential deal alive with him, I suggest you do what he says."

The Barracuda replied, "I get you. We'll catch up some other time then."

She heard the Barracuda walk back to his room and slam the door behind him. She then heard him cursing out the man who she had gotten into a fight with. As she drifted off to sleep all she could think was that Ben owed her big time for having her put up with the criminals in the next suite over.

The pilot laid down and smiled when she thought about taking down the bodyguard who had tried to stab that man. The more she thought about it, the more she realized that she had not felt a rush or the sense of satisfaction like that since she was in the Air Force. Isabell sighed, as she realized that she might want more from Ben in more ways than one.

She walked over to the mirror and took a good look at herself. "Face it, girl," she muttered aloud to her image. "If you are going to have a greater sense of making a difference in the world or of being more than just Ben's pilot, you are going to have to have to have a serious talk with him."

CHAPTER 13

As the sun started to set over Port City, Ben Watkins was pulling another exo-suit over his bruised and battered body. The very act of putting the suit on was painful as it pressed against the bruises that littered his torso and back. When he was finally dressed, Raptor reloaded his bandoliers, gauntlets, and his drone.

He then climbed onto his motorcycle, activated his drone, and drove down through the storm drain system adjacent to his lair. He had nearly reached the end of the tunnel when he saw the last rays of sunlight dip down and cast the city in darkness. He cursed as he knew he had to hurry to reach the Barracuda's house before Charles did.

Ben Watkins had sent the Barracuda to Las Vegas, but the mobster would undoubtedly have left several men to guard his house. When Charles arrived there, he would try to make his way inside to kill the crime lord.

Even with their boss out of town the men at the Barracuda's house would protect his property at all costs. After having witnessed what Charles could do firsthand, Raptor had no doubt that the revenant would massacre the Barracuda's men. To make matters worse, if the crime lord returned home to find his men slaughtered, he would likely blame a rival gang and retaliate in kind.

Raptor had hoped to save lives by getting the Barracuda and some of his men out of town, but if he didn't arrive at the house before Charles and Retribution did, he knew his actions could end up costing more lives than they saved.

Thirty minutes later, Raptor arrived at the Barracuda's house. The hero had the drone fly over the residence for reconnaissance. It was clear from the video feed and the scans the drone had completed that Charles had not yet arrived to start his attack. The thermal scans also indicated that there were three guards in the house that he would need to incapacitate before Charles attacked.

When the hero saw that the three men were all gathered together in the den, Raptor smiled and said to himself, "At least they are making it easy for me, with them all being in one place."

Raptor climbed off his motorcycle and quickly got to work. He had learned from his last encounter with Charles and Retribution that the revenant was using the city's storm drain system to move around. The hero used this knowledge to his advantage by placing motion detectors and electric shock traps on the interior of the two storm drains on the Barracuda's street. When Charles tried to move the storm drain grating, not only would Raptor know that the monster was nearby, but his trap would also buy him a few extra moments to prepare for facing Charles again.

With the traps and motion detectors in place, Raptor moved onto the house. The first thing he did was to approach one of the cameras the bookie had installed as part of his security system.

When he was within a few feet of the device the hero gave a command to the supercomputer embedded in his visor: "Hack into the home security system for 42 Evergreen Lane." Less than a minute later, his visor indicated that he had access to the home security system. He whispered, "Turn off the home security system." His visor immediately indicated that the house's home security system had been shut down.

Raptor fired his grappling hook onto the roof and used it to scale the Barracuda's house. He then walked over to the chimney. The hero took a tear gas sphere off his bandolier and dropped it down the smokestack. The three guards the Barracuda had left at his house were sitting in the den right below playing cards. When the tear gas sphere hit the unlit fireplace, it exploded and filled the first floor with the suffocating gas.

The three guards immediately started coughing. They then tried to get to the back door to exit the house. Raptor waited for the first two to come outside, then he dropped down on them from the roof. The crime fighter hit the two men like a ton of bricks, instantly knocking them out on impact. Raptor then turned to see the third man coughing and rubbing his eyes as he ran out the door. The caped crusader walked up to him and knocked him unconscious with a single punch.

With all three guards unconscious on the back porch, the hero dragged them away from the house and then tied them up. Then he dashed into the house and made his way back to the Barracuda's office. He walked over to the mobster's 'computer and turned it on.

The hero commanded into his visor, "Initiate action to clone the contents of the computer's hard drive."

Next, he walked over to the picture he had seen on the wall and designated it as a likely safe cover during his visit as Ben Watkins. The hero took the picture off the wall and found the safe he was looking for. He moved toward its metal door and leaned his head against it.

Raptor then gave another command to his visor, "Activate helmet's auditory enhancements."

He then placed the ear of his helmet against the side of the safe and listened as he slowly turned its dial. Three minutes later he had cracked the safe. He took out its contents to find the mobster's ledger. A thorough perusal of the ledger provided proof that the Barracuda had taken part in hundreds of illegal gambling operations. The ledger was more than enough to put the mobster in jail for decades.

As he finished examining the journal a message flashed across his visor that the computer's hard drive had been completely copied to his servers back in his lair.

The hero took the ledger and the mobster's computer and placed them at the feet of the unconscious guards.

He had placed the evidence to indict the Barracuda in plain sight so that when the police arrived, they would have legal access to it. That was when his visor alerted him that one of his motion detectors had been activated. The hero quickly ran to the front of the house to see sparks lighting up the storm drain on the right side of the street.

Raptor sprinted across the lawn, jumped onto his motorcycle, and pulled it behind a line of bushes in the Barracuda's side yard. He turned to his right to see the storm drain that was filled with sparks only a moment ago lifted off its moors and moved into the street. The masked detective then saw the deformed body of Charles Donnor crawl out of the manhole. The hulking revenant's body was smoking from the shock Raptor's trap had given him.

The crime fighter did not see Retribution alongside Charles with his naked eye.

He spoke into his visor, "Activate electromagnetic view." When the requested view came on, Raptor could see the petite form of Retribution floating besides Charles.

The vigilante waited for the undead murder-victim-turned-murderer to walk on to the Barracuda's lawn. That was when he spoke into his visor, "Move drone control to gauntlets."

Raptor lowered his hands, and as he did so the drone descended from the sky. He then slid his thumbs along his index fingers which activated the flood lights attached to the front of the airborne weapon.

Charles Donnor stopped in his tracks when the burst of light shone in his eyes. Raptor then clenched his fists to activate the drone's high powered machine guns. Charles' body was pelted with a barrage of bullets and other projectiles. The ferocity of the attack was such that even the monstrous revenant was forced to take several steps back. The barrage lasted for nearly a full minute before Raptor halted his attack.

When the drone had finally stopped firing, Charles' body was riddled with bullet holes, but the undead colossus was still standing.

Retribution made herself visible and called out in her ghostly voice, "We figured you were here when Charles got that shock in the storm drain. You might as well show yourself. After the beating you took yesterday, I'm surprised you would show up here to try and protect another murderer."

The crime fighter pulled his motorcycle out from behind the bushes. "The Barracuda's not here," he said. "In fact, he is several thousand miles away."

Retribution looked intently at the house. Raptor guessed that she was using her supernatural powers to confirm what he had said.

The goddess sighed and then looked at Raptor. "All you have done is delay the inevitable. Charles and I will either wait for the mobster to return or we shall track him down. No matter where he is in the world, we will find him." She shifted her gaze to Raptor's drone and said, "At least you have learned that even your most powerful weapon is useless against those I have granted the power to gain their revenge."

"I had to try," Raptor replied with a grin.

Retribution floated several steps toward Raptor. "Enjoy the small inconvenience you have caused me tonight," she said. "For in two days when I come for you, it will be your last night on Earth. Then once you are gone Charles will have his revenge, as will the countless other souls who cry out for vengeance in this city."

"I better get going then, and get my affairs in order," the hero responded. He then gave another command into his visor: "Reactivate house alarm system."

The command caused the house's security tech to turn on. The reactivated system sent out alarms which would bring the police to find the tied-up men and the evidence Raptor had left in plain view for them. With the alarm activated, Raptor sped down the street as his drone followed him from above.

When the hero was out of site Retribution said to Charles, "Return to where the water drains. I shall check on this house daily. When its master returns, we shall return also, and you shall have your revenge. As for me, I have other matters to attend to tonight."

Charles grunted and started walking back toward the storm drain.

As Raptor was driving down the street he spoke into his visor, "Activate tracker." A display appeared in the hero's visor showing a target moving away from the Barracuda's house. *Good. I figured that he and Retribution would not notice a tracker entering his body at the same time as all those bullets. Now I know exactly where Charles is at all times.*

The hero then commanded into his visor, "Call the manager of the Watkins Hotel in Las Vegas."

When the manager answered the phone, Raptor used his Ben Watkins voice to give him instructions. "This is Ben Watkins. I need you to offer my apologies to the men staying in my penthouse. Please tell them that I will not be able to meet them as I had hoped and that I will fly them home tomorrow. Please also inform them that for this inconvenience I will double the original sum I promised them. Further inform them that they are welcome to use that sum as a line of credit in the casino, or that I can pay them when they return home tomorrow. Please notify my pilot of this decision as well."

The manager indicated that he would relay the message and then he hung up. With his first several objectives for the night successfully completed, Raptor set his sights on the American History Museum.

As he drove through the city streets, Raptor's mind was focused on the potentially, dangerous series of events he had set into motion. With what he left for the police; they would arrest the Barracuda as soon as he returned home.

The hero would have to answer some questions as Ben Watkins regarding what the mobster was doing at his hotel, but that could easily be explained by saying he had legitimate interest in dealing with the man until he found out about his criminal activities. This story would be supported by his quick removal of the Barracuda from his hotel and why he never flew out to Las Vegas to meet with the man.

The much more dangerous potential consequence of Raptor's actions was the possibility of Charles going after the Barracuda while he was in police custody. The test with his drone tonight had proven how durable the revenant was. If the barrage from the military grade drone was unable to do any serious damage to Charles, then there was nothing the Port City police department had in their arsenal that would stop the walking dead man either.

This meant that Raptor would have to find some way to neutralize both Charles and Retribution before the crime lord was taken into custody. The thought occurred to him that he might be able to use Charles' pursuit of the Barracuda to his advantage. If he had the mobster himself, then, Charles would come to him.

The monster had already proved that he was much more powerful than Raptor, but in any battle if one could choose the battleground ahead of time, and prepare for the upcoming encounter, then they had an advantage. Raptor knew that against a juggernaut like Charles he would need every advantage he could gain.

He gave the following command into his visor: "Delete any record of the flight plans for Ben Watkins' personal plane over the next three days. Additionally, alert me four hours prior to the plane landing in Port City in its return flight from Las Vegas."

The message, "Command accepted and alert set." flashed across Raptor's visor.

The second thought that occupied his mind was Retribution's continual threats that she would be coming for him. So far, the people she had brought back to life had only attacked those who they felt were responsible for their deaths. In Charles' case, the people he was attacking all seemed to have a direct connection to his murder. Torrol's actions were a bit more clouded, as either he or the dogs he was combined with blamed the people who were betting on the sport for their deaths as well as the man who had actually killed him.

It was this thought that bothered Raptor. He was unaware of how his actions as either Raptor or Ben Watkins had caused the death of anyone. In his latter identity, he fought hard to make sure that the technologies he developed were always used in a non-lethal capacity.

As Raptor he had put numerous criminals in jail, but he had never killed anyone. Some of the people he had put in jail were later murdered by other inmates for their actions. Even then, could the person who was murdered see that as his fault? Even if they did blame him for their deaths, would a goddess like Retribution support a desire for revenge to extend that far?

Raptor still had no idea what criteria Retribution was using to grant people the means to exact their revenge. Did those who caused the wronged person's death have to violate what she saw as some moral code? Or, was it simply that the person who died blamed a certain number of people for their deaths without regard as to whether their actions could be seen as morally right or not?

All these queries came down to the question of judicial punishment or vengeance. As Raptor pulled his motorcycle to a stop in front of the American History Museum, he hoped that either he or someone – or perhaps *something* else – could prove to Retribution that there was a distinction between the two.

The hero dismounted from his bike, aimed his gauntlet at the top of the museum, and fired his grappling line at it. Once the line was secure, he used it to scale the side of the building all the way to the top. After he reached the roof, the hero quickly made his way over to one of the access panels to the museum's power supply.

He gave another command to his visor: "Access museum security system."

The tech at the museum was much more sophisticated than the Barracuda's home security system. It took the vigilante's supercomputer nearly fifteen minutes to hack into the system and shut it down.

Once the system was down, Raptor picked the lock to the door and entered the museum. The crime fighter made his way down to the Ulysses S. Grant exhibit, where he walked past several statues and paintings of the former general and president. As he was making his way through the gallery, Raptor saw the many positive and terrible actions Grant had taken in his life. The crime fighter wondered how many revenants Retribution would have sent after Grant if he happened to have fallen in her sight.

When the hero walked up to the sword that Grant had used at Appomattox Courthouse to end the Civil War, he knew he had found a symbol of Justice.

This was the sword that had effectively put an official end to slavery in the U.S., one of the most just causes that any person could have undertaken.

As Raptor grabbed the sword, he said to himself, "That's the difference between justice and vengeance. Justice allows a person the chance to rise above their mistakes and still have a positive influence on the world. Vengeance only punishes them."

With Grant's sword in hand, the vigilante made his way back through the exhibit. Raptor searched for the last item he needed to perform the ritual to call Nemesis: a whip that was an instrument of justice or vengeance. The hero knew this would be the most difficult item to find, as whips were typically used by those in power to punish the people beneath them; throughout history, only rarely was a whip used as an instrument of justice.

Raptor decided he might have to find some way to improvise the whip needed for the ritual to summon Nemesis. When he reached the roof, the hero relocked the door he had come in through.

A crack of thunder sounded overhead as a streak of lightning flashed across the sky. Raptor looked up to see a torrent or rain coming down from above. He smiled as he felt like the storm mirrored his current state of mind. The usually calm and focused hero found himself stealing items from various public places in an attempt to stop a goddess from inflicting vengeance as opposed to dispensing justice. The actions he was taking to stop Retribution's killing spree did not sit well with the hero's conscience. His mind was like the storm taking place around him: disjointed and not unsettled.

Raptor pushed his internal reflections aside and used his grappling cord to make his way back down the side of the building. When he reached his motorcycle, he placed the sword in a special carrying compartment he had attached to the vehicle. He then made his way back to his lair to ready himself for the upcoming battle between himself and Retribution.

CHAPTER 14

With her thirst for vengeance on the Barracuda unfulfilled due to the Raptor's interference, Retribution moved onto another soul-seeking revenge. She appeared at the construction site where Chester Mansfield had been murdered the night before. She floated over the slab of concrete with a large hole in it and landed next to a large mound of dirt piled alongside the shattered concrete.

She looked at the concrete and then shifted her gaze to the sky above. She moved her hands back and forth several times and then pointed down at the mound of dirt. As she did so, a deluge of rain fell from the sky and pounded on to the knoll. The unrelenting rain caused the mound of dirt to turn into mud.

As the rain continued to fall on it the mound of mud began to fall apart and slide away. Retribution was standing next to the embankment when she made a circular motion above her head and then pointed again at the newly laid foundation.

When her hands fell a bolt of lightning streaked down from the sky and struck the dried cement. The bolt danced over the mound of wet dirt and as it faded away something began to move beneath the soaked soil.

Retribution repeated the same hand waving motion causing a second bolt of lightning to come down and strike the same target. As the electrical energies cascaded over the mound a second time, the concrete suddenly exploded, and a monstrous figure emerged from it.

The creature was nearly seven feet tall and composed of solid concrete. It had a humanoid shape with a head, torso, legs, arms, hands, and a completely featureless face. The monster's face only gave the slightest hint of a brow and an indent where its mouth should have been. The creature looked at Retribution and it moaned as more lightning streaked over its head and the rain continued to come down in a torrent.

The goddess looked at the creature she had created and smiled before speaking aloud.

"Chester Mansfield. A small man who lived his entire life afraid of those larger and more powerful than himself. You died on this very spot when Agents Desopo and McKinney buried you in the liquid rock. I have brought you back as a golem using the very substance, they killed you with. Now you have the power to take revenge on those who murdered you."

She flew closer to the golem and looked into where his eyes should have been. Then she said "They are not the only ones you desire revenge on though, are they? Ben Watkins, your former employer. Had he simply accepted your proposal none of this would have happened. Then, as Raptor he prevented you from saving yourself by obtaining the equipment that would have placated the agents, didn't he?"

The golem that had once been Chester Mansfield nodded in response.

Retribution started floating away and she gestured for the monster to follow her. "Come, tonight we shall pay Agent McKinney a visit."

The rain was falling hard as agent Larry McKinney drove his car to the warehouse district down by the docks. He stopped in front of one of the bay doors with a ramp on it for the address he was given and honked his horn three times. A few seconds after he had beeped, the bay door opened up and a well-built man was waving for McKinney to drive into the warehouse. The secret agent nodded and pulled his car into the building where he was meeting the contacts from the failed Mansfield contract. He pulled the car to a stop as the large steel doors to the warehouse closed behind him.

As McKinney opened his car door several men of mixed origins came out from behind various shelving units and pallets. McKinney nodded to a man wearing a New York Yankees baseball cap and then walked around to his trunk. The agent opened it up as the man in the cap walked over to the car.

The latter individual peered into the back of the trunk and shook his head. "These are not the weapons we were promised," he said. "Desopo promised us advanced experimental weapons. These are standard weapons."

McKinney reached into the trunk and pulled out an assault rifle. "These are the newest version of the M-16 rifle," he told the buyer. "We are also providing you with armor piercing rounds. Based on the latest intel we have on your opposition these weapons should give you a significant advantage over them."

The man in the cap's eyes flared with anger. "These weapons will help us win skirmishes. We are trying to win wars! We were promised weapons that could win a war! Desopo said he would provide us with technology that would cripple the government's operating systems!"

McKinney endeavored to remain calm. "Desopo is deeply regretful that we were unable to obtain the technology he promised you. He would like to continue doing business with you and to support your cause. As such, he is willing to sell you these weapons at a significant discount."

The man in cap began to scream as he pulled a handgun and pointed it at McKinney. "These weapons will do nothing but get us killed! We are still greatly outnumbered by the government! Desopo said that he had technology which could help us win battles and bring the government to a halt! These weapons will accomplish neither of those objectives!"

McKinney looked around to see that over a half dozen men all had handguns pointed at him. He held his hands up. "Look, fellas. This is not something you want to do. If you kill me, Desopo will rain hell down on your guys like you can't believe." He gestured to weapons in his trunk. "These are top of the line weapons. Why don't we…"

McKinney's thought was cut short by a banging on the bay door.

The man in the baseball cap glared at McKinney. "You are seeking to ambush us?"

McKinney shook his head. "No, I'm here alone. I have no idea who that is."

The banging grew louder, and sections of the steel door began to bulge out as if something had struck them. The man in the baseball cap motioned for one of his men to go over to the door and see what was going on. The man slowly walked to the entrance and when he reached it a large concrete arm smashed through the thick metal.

The man screamed and began firing at the arm as a second concrete arm punched through the door. The two rock-hard limbs tore through the bay door as if it were paper and created an opening for the golem to walk into the warehouse.

"Jesus, what in the hell is that?" McKinney screamed.

The man who was standing by the bay door continued to fire at the golem. The stone giant turned to the man, reached out with his long arm, and wrapped his massive hand around the terrorist's head. The golem squeezed causing bits of brain and skull to squirt between his fingers as he crushed the terrorist's head like a grape.

The man in the baseball cap screamed, "Kill that monster!" The gathered terrorists began firing on the concrete revenant as McKinney loaded the assault rifle in his hand.

The golem walked through the small arms fire from the terrorists as if their bullets were nothing more than a gentle rain. He grabbed another man near him by the right arm and left leg. The mythical beast then lifted the man over his head and with one pull tore him in half.

Three more men ran up to the golem and started firing on him at point blank range. Despite their closer proximity, the terrorist weapons still had no effect on the monster.

The golem moved with a speed that defied his size, weight, and composition. In a flurry of movement, the monster struck one man in the chest shattering his ribcage and crushing his heart and lungs. The concrete giant then spun around and brought his fists crashing down on another man, smashing him to a pulp.

The monster next turned to a third man, grabbed him by the neck, and tossed him upwards. The thrown man hit the ceiling with such force that every bone in his body shattered on impact. His limp and broken form fell to the floor with a sickening splat.

McKinney was standing next to the man in the baseball cap and his two remaining guards. The CIA agent screamed as he opened fire with the assault rifle. Pieces of the golem's concrete "skin" chipped away as the armor piercing bullets struck it. The impact of the bullets was such that it forced the monster to move backward from the assault.

After McKinney had emptied the clip, he inspected the damage he had inflicted upon the golem's stone-like shell. He and the three remaining terrorists watched in stunned silence as bullet holes the size of golf balls filled themselves back in with fresh concrete.

McKinney looked at the men around him and shouted, "Quick, grab some of the guns from the trunk!"

The terrorists were reaching for the firearms when the golem sprinted across the room. The concrete colossus grabbed a terrorist in each hand and then slammed their bodies together, sending a spray of blood, bones, and organs all over the car, McKinney, and the man in the baseball cap.

The golem then grabbed McKinney, pushed him to the floor, and used his foot to pin him down without killing him. The man in the cap pointed an assault rifle at golem but before he could fire, the monster grabbed the helpless guy and lifted him into the air.

The golem first grabbed the man's right leg and snapped it like a twig. He then repeated the process to the man's other leg and arms. The victim with the baseball cap was still screaming as the golem shaped his broken body into a square and then placed him in the trunk of the car. The terrorist continued to scream in pain as the monster closed the trunk on his mangled body.

The monster then turned its featureless face down to look at McKinney. For nearly a minute the golem just stared at the corrupt CIA man. The agent tried to free himself from under the monster's foot but once he realized he was trapped he screamed, "Come on then, finish me off already!"

A beautiful blonde woman wearing a black halter top, a mini skirt, and a long black jacket with a sword attached to her hip, floated out from behind the golem. She landed parallel to McKinney and then crouched down next to his head.

She whispered into his ear, "He will kill you, Agent McKinney, but your death won't be quick like those other men who stood between you and him. As you made his death slow and painful, so shall your death be as well."

"What are you talking about?" McKinney cried. "I didn't kill this thing! I've never seen anything like it in my life!"

Retribution shook her head and replied, "Let me peel back the covering you put on his face. Then maybe you will recognize him."

The goddess waved her toward the golem's countenance, causing the concrete that covered it to recede and reveal the dust-covered face of Chester Mansfield.

McKinney shook his head in shock and horror. "No, you're dead! This can't be real!"

"I assure you this is quite real," Retribution replied, "and your death is going to take a really long time." She looked up at Chester as the concrete slowly reformed over his face. "We have nothing else to do tonight. What do you think? An increase of five pounds of pressure every fifteen minutes? That should slowly crush him to death over the next five hours or so."

McKinney screamed as Retribution looked down at him and grinned. "Once we have squeezed the life out of this murderer, we shall turn our attention to his superior." She turned her back toward the golem. "I have found the location of where he is currently residing. He has many of his soldiers there but if they decide to interfere, they shall meet the same fate as those who foolishly stood in the way of your vengeance here."

The vengeance goddess moved over to a nearby window and looked at the night sky before speaking aloud again.

"Tomorrow night we shall make our move on Agent Desopo. With the deaths of two federal agents the city will take notice of our actions. Soon the masses will be aware that all who commit wrongs on others in Port City shall feel the wrath of Retribution!"

CHAPTER 15

Ben Watkins awoke the next morning and turned on the news to see a report about the grizzly massacre that had occurred at a warehouse roughly five miles from the various such locations he used as cover for his base of operations. When the reporter said that the bodies in the warehouse appeared to have been crushed and torn to pieces, Ben called his office and told them he would be out for the day. He then dressed and drove his recreational motorcycle to his warehouse.

Once he had reached his warehouse, he took a secret passage down to his lair and walked over to where he kept his bird-themed helmet. Ben placed the covering over his head and immediately got to work.

"Access police computers and show me the information for the warehouse murders that occurred last night at 50 River Drive."

A few seconds later, a visual display appeared in front of Raptor showing him pictures from the warehouse, as well as written reports on the crime. The masked crusader first looked at the crime scene photos. The reporter on the news had greatly understated how gruesome the scene truly was. The men there were not just torn apart; they were clearly crushed to death by something or someone with incredible strength.

One photo showed where a man had been killed by being slammed into the ceiling and then fell back to the floor.

The body of a second man looked as if he had been slowly crushed to death. The latter's torso was completely collapsed but the blood that had come out of him was pooled around his mouth and nose. If he had been crushed quickly there would have been a large area covered in his blood. The photo Raptor was looking at revealed a man who had an increasing amount of weight placed on his chest that likely caused his lungs to fill with blood, thereby slowly suffocating him as he was crushed to death.

Raptor then moved onto a photo of the trunk of a car filled with military grade weapons that was left at the site.

He said to himself, "This wasn't a gang hit or some kind of turf war. No gang or organized crime family would have left weapons like that behind."

The next set of crime scene photos showed what looked like shattered concrete all over the floor. Some of the rocky chunks that were left had bullet holes in them. Raptor carefully looked at the backgrounds of each of the photos and saw no sign of any large sections of concrete that had suffered damage during the carnage. As usual, the hero was reluctant to jump to a conclusion without sufficient evidence, but he was starting to think that the massacre at the warehouse may have been the work of Retribution.

The hero barked out another command into his visor: "Show me the movements of Charles Donnor for the last ten hours."

His visor brought up the requested info from the tracker he had placed in the revenant the night before. Raptor spoke aloud to himself (as was his habit) while he looked at the information.

"Charles seems to have stayed deep in the drain system all night after our encounter. He really didn't move much at all. If this is Retribution's work, it seems to indicate she has created another revenant."

Raptor then turned his attention to the written crime reports. The first item of note was that the body of a man found in the trunk of the car belonged to a suspected well-funded anarchist group from overseas. The group was known to be involved in attempts to undermine and overthrow their own government.

Raptor was reading through the rest of the report when he received an update from one of the detectives on the scene. The update indicated that the car and the weapons which had been taken into custody were to be turned over to an Agent Desopo, who would be arriving at the station around 10:00 am.

The vigilante sighed. "Chester Mansfield breaks into my office with two men who appear to be CIA operatives. The potential operatives are immediately taken into federal custody after they are arrested. The police have been unable to locate Mansfield, an individual whose background does not suggest he would have any idea how to drop off the grid.

"A massacre, possibly involving Retribution, takes place in a warehouse where weapons were being picked up by the CIA" He shook his head. "If there is a connection between Mansfield, the CIA, and Retribution then finding Mansfield may be more of a priority than I had originally thought."

He checked his watch to see that it currently read 9:00 am. He then looked at the weather report for the day.

Raptor commented into his visor, "Trying to follow a CIA operative, on a motorcycle, in the middle of day, without him noticing, would be a difficult task. There is still a good deal of cloud cover in the sky from last night's storms. The cloud cover could represent an excellent opportunity to follow Agent Desopo from the air without being detected."

He looked over in the direction of his drone and said, "Activate drone, and set for remote control piloting through my gauntlets."

At the sound of the command, the drone sprung to life and hovered in the air. Raptor placed his gauntlets on his hands and shifted them from side to side. As he made the motions with his hands the drone shifted accordingly. With the cavorting device fully under his control, the hero initiated the drones' stealth mode, and then guided it through the tunnels and out into the sky.

An hour later the drone was hovering over the Port City 12th precinct. The vigilante had the drone well covered in the clouds so that neither the police nor the CIA agent were likely to notice it. Raptor had the device's cameras focused on the entrance to the precinct's evidence room as it was the most likely place for the agent to pick up the weapons in question.

At two minutes after ten, the drone's camera filmed a black car with no plates pulling into the precinct parking lot. Raptor watched through his visor as a tall, well-built man with a crew cut and wearing a black suit stepped out of the vehicle. The man's appearance and the way he walked all confirmed that he was indeed a government agent.

Raptor spoke into his visor, "Check CIA records for facial recognition."

The computer program he had inserted into the CIA database began trying to find the identity of the man in question. The vigilante knew that even his program would take a little time to work its way unnoticed through the CIA database. He let the program do its job and refocused his attention on the live video feed.

The agent was in the evidence room for a good half an hour. When he finally came out, he was followed by two police officers who were carrying large trash bags. From the way the bags were shaped and the manner in which the officers were carrying them, Raptor assumed that the contents were the guns in question.

The agent opened the back of his trunk and the officers placed the bags in it. He then climbed into his car and left the police station.

Raptor had his drone follow the agent throughout the metropolis and finally out of the city limits. The agent drove for another twenty minutes after exiting Port City and finally stopped at a motel on the outskirts.

When he saw the motel, Raptor had his drone fly a circle over it so he could better understand exactly what kind of establishment the agent was staying at. When the hero saw a half, dozen pitch black cars without license plates in the parking lot, he knew he was looking at a CIA hub. Despite the drone's stealth mode, several agents came out of their rooms and were looking up in the general direction of the airborne device. Raptor guessed that even if they couldn't see the drone on radar and the cloud cover was obscuring their view, they still had people looking at the sky who had seen something they thought was odd.

Raptor slowly guided his drone through the clouds and away from the hub. The crime fighter knew that if he was going to find Chester Mansfield the most likely place to do so was in that hub. The issue now was devising a way to infiltrate the building, find Mansfield, and question him without getting into a confrontation with ten or more CIA agents.

Raptor switched the drone over to autopilot and directed it to fly back to his lair. He then brought up the video recording of the area around the hub so that he could look for methods in which he could approach the CIA operation.

The location where the CIA had set up their operation was strategically picked on their part. The seemingly innocuous motel was in the middle of a large field that extended for several miles around it in a complete 360 degrees. From what Raptor could see in the feed from the drone, there was no cover that he could use while approaching the hub from the field.

There was only one road to or from the motel. The single road access gave the agents in the building a clear line of sight for any vehicles heading toward them. The vigilante immediately dismissed the road as a viable access point due to its visibility.

Raptor was considering other methods to approach the hub when his algorithm came back with a hit on the facial recognition search. The name and picture of Agent Michael Desopo appeared inside the hero's visor.

"At least now I know which agent to go after," he noted to himself.

The masked crusader switched off the facial recognition program as a warning flashed across his screen, indicating that Isabell was on her way back from Las Vegas with the Barracuda and his men.

The hero spoke into his visor, "Connect me with Isabell on the plane."

A moment later Raptor could hear his pilot's voice through his visor. "Listen, Ben, you owe me big time for this one. Flying these jerks out there was no big deal but hanging around with them and keeping their hands off me was going a little beyond the call of duty.

"One of them became violent with two other customers at the club. I had to intervene, which resulted in the thug ending up with a broken nose and a couple broken fingers. I'm glad you decided to call them back early, but you owe me for this and I'm not talking about money. I fully plan to take this out on you in the gym tonight, in what I can promise you will be a heated sparring session."

Raptor laughed and replied, "I think I am going to need your skills as a pilot tonight as opposed to a sparring session. However, I also think we are going to need to incapacitate these guys when they get off the plane. You're more than welcome to help me knock these guys out if you can do it without them seeing you."

Isabell's voice came back with a tinge of excitement. "So, I take it you want me to land at the airport and then take these guys to the warehouse on the helicopter?"

"Yes. Tell them that as part of his apology for not being able to make it out to Las Vegas, Ben Watkins will fly them to his house for some drinks. I'll have the drone pretend to force you down by the warehouse, so they don't make a connection between Watkins and Raptor. Once they are off the plane, we can both pay these men back for the way they treated you."

Isabell giggled. "I love it that you think you need to stand up for me. Get yourself ready, we'll be there in a few hours."

Raptor severed the connection with Isabell and then reached out to Eric.

As usual, the driver was quick to answer his employer's call. "Yes, sir."

"I need you to come to the warehouse, with a car that can fit at least three people in the back. I also need you to make sure the car has a little speed to it in case you need to get away from anything."

"As you wish, sir."

111

Two hours later Eric was at the warehouse with a very unique looking limousine Ben had never seen before.

Ben walked out of the building when he saw the strange vehicle. "That's quite a car you have there," he said. The industrialist walked around the car and took a close look at it. "It's durable. I can see bulletproofing on the windows and exterior." He then inspected the bottom portion of the vehicle. "The tires look as if it would take a high-powered rifle to pierce them." He turned to Eric. ``What about the speed?"

"Zero to eighty in sixty seconds," Eric replied. "It also has the ability to produce a nitrous bust if needed."

Ben placed his hand on the shoulder of his friend and driver and said, "Listen, I am going to put you in a dangerous position on three fronts. First, you will be transporting a trio of known mobsters. The good news about them is they will be unconscious for part of the ride and restrained for the entirety. Secondly, at least one of the men you will be transporting is being hunted by an undead juggernaut who is under the thrall of a seemingly all-powerful goddess."

Eric's eyes went wide. "Well, that's something new."

Ben handed Eric a tracker display and said, "On the bright side, I did manage to get a tracker into the revenant. So, at least you'll know if he's getting close to you."

Eric took the small device. "Well, that's comforting," he said. He then beamed a sarcastic smile as he looked back at Ben. "You said there was a third front to deal with as well?"

"While you're driving this car full of criminals with a monster after you, you'll be heading to a CIA hub. It looks like a motel. I need you to drive around it, taking pictures and to draw some of the agents in the hub into chasing you."

Ben changed his voice to a more serious tone. "Eric, I know that I am really asking a lot of you here. I need to keep the Barracuda and his crew alive and, on the move, so Charles and Retribution can't get to them. I also need to get into that CIA hub because they broke into my office with Mansfield, and it looks like Retribution may be after them as well."

He looked his friend directly in the eye. "I'm going to tell you the same thing I told Isabell. If you want to back out of this, that's perfectly fine. I will not think any less of you."

"Mobsters, undead slashers, the CIA, and an all-powerful goddess. This will be a walk in the park compared to one day in Afghanistan."

"Thank you, Eric." He then looked at his watch. "Isabell is going to be here soon. We need to get out of sight and get the drone in the air."

A half hour later Isabell was flying over the river near the warehouse, with the Barracuda and his men in the back of the vehicle.

When they were over the waterway the Barracuda was looking out over the city when he saw something large and black flying toward them. He pointed out the window and called out to Isabell, "What the heck is that thing? It looks like it's coming right for us."

Isabell took the gangster's question as her cue to start playing her part. She looked at her radar and said, "What thing? I don't have anything on radar." She then looked out the side of the window and screamed, "Oh hell! It's that vigilante they call Raptor! I've heard stories from other pilots of him using a drone to force aircraft down when they were carrying people he was after!" She shouted back to the Barracuda, "You guys haven't done anything that would cause Raptor to be after you, have you?"

The Barracuda was starting to panic. "You've got to lose that thing! We can't let Raptor get a hold of us."

Isabell watched as a stream of what she knew were blank bullets fired well wide of her helicopter. She shouted, "That is an armed military drone! This is an unarmed transport helicopter! We can't outrun that thing and we sure as hell can't outgun it!" She looked down at the warehouse below her. "It's forcing us down in that warehouse parking lot! I either land there or it shoots us down!"

The Barracuda continued to panic. "Aw, hell no. *Hell no!*" He looked at his bodyguards. "It's time for you two to earn your pay!"

Isabell landed the helicopter and turned off its blades as the drone circled overhead. When the blades stopped moving, she screamed, "Now, quickly make a run for it!" She then reached under her chair and grabbed a gas mask as the Barracuda and his men jumped out of the copter.

Isabell pulled the mask over her face as a sphere flew out of seemingly nowhere and exploded to release a cloud of tear gas.

The Barracuda and his men were choking on the gas as Raptor dashed into the cloud. The hero hit the bodyguard whose nose and finger Isabell had broken with an uppercut that rendered him unconscious. He then spun around and struck the second bodyguard with a roundhouse punch that knocked him out.

The Barracuda was wandering through the noxious cloud when Isabell jumped on top of his back and wrapped her arm around his neck. The pilot pressed her face – which was still covered in a gas mask – tightly on the back of the gangster's neck and then used her legs to trip him. The Barracuda fell hard and face-first on the ground. The gangster struggled for a minute but the combined factors of the gas, his fall, and Isabell's choke hold were too much for the bookie and he slowly passed out.

As the gas cleared away Raptor took out zip ties and secured the arms and legs of the Barracuda and his men.

He then dragged the criminals away from the helicopter and the lingering remnants of the tear gas he had used. As the hero was doing this Eric pulled the customized limo over to the pile of unconscious men. He opened the door for Raptor and threw them into the back seat of the car.

The vigilante looked at his driver and said, "We've got about two hours until nightfall. I'll give these men a sedative to keep them from struggling. Keep the shield between the passengers and the driver up so they can't see who you are."

"It's two hours until we need you to drive to the CIA hub. In that time, keep the car moving and keep an eye on the tracker I gave you. If you see Charles getting close to you, drive away quickly. If you find that you can't get away from him, if there is nothing else you can do to save the lives of these men, just leave them and run. There is no need for you to die trying to protect men like these."

"I shall not leave them to die unless there is no other option. But I shall not die trying to defend them."

Isabell walked over to the two men and asked, "What part am I playing in this CIA raid/monster hunt?"

Raptor turned toward his pilot. "There's no way to approach the hub from the ground, and they have radar for low flying aircraft. I am going to have you fly me at cruising altitude so the guys on radar don't think anything of the aircraft flying over them. I'll jump from the plane and use my cape's parachute function to land on the ground. My exo-suit's stealth function will keep me off their radar and hopefully I won't have to much ground to cover after I land."

Isabell sighed. "Eric has a car full of gangsters and a monster after him and all I'm doing is flying over an old motel." She turned and walked into the warehouse.

Eric called over to his employer, "I shall get moving, sir. I will do the drive through the motel parking lot in exactly two hours."

Raptor nodded. "Good. Thank you and stay safe."

Eric then got into his car and drove away with the Barracuda and his men in tow.

Raptor tried to calm down and followed Isabell into the warehouse. As he entered the building, he took off his helmet. He saw Isabell standing by the back of the warehouse looking at the scales he had taken from the statue of Lady Justice and the sword of Ulysses S. Grant."

She heard him walking up behind her and said, "Are you starting some kind of museum or something?"

"Those things may be the method through which we can finally stop Retribution. Apparently, with the scales, and then a sword and whip that represent justice, we can call the goddess Nemesis. If that ceremony works, I am hoping that we can appeal to her to stop Retribution's killing spree. It's a long shot but right now it's all we have."

"What are you going to use for a whip that represents justice?"

"I haven't figured that part out yet." He changed his tone of voice. "Isabell, your role in this mission is a vital one. I don't have anyone else who can fly the plane."

She turned around to look at her employer face-to-face. "It's not like I don't understand that, Ben. I know that my part is crucial in this mission. I know that I play a vital role for you. It's just... I used to be a fighter pilot. I used to be on the front lines. When we were taking those men down outside, when I was in Vegas and stopped that man from stabbing someone... I felt like I was making more of a difference."

Ben walked closer to her. "Is that what you really want? More dangerous missions?"

Isabell nodded her head. "I want more. I need more. I joined the Air Force to make a difference in the world. To stop evil people like terrorists and fascist regimes. When you told me about what you were doing, about how your family was taken from you by evil people, I knew this is where I was meant to be. I knew that I had found someone who understood the drive in me... the drive to make a real hands-on difference in the world."

She took a few steps closer to Ben before continuing. "The work we have done together. It means a lot to me, but I want to make a bigger difference. I want to be out there with you on the front lines."

Ben shook his head. "You don't know what you're asking. It's not just gangsters out there. It's giant monsters, undead slashers, and ancient gods." He gestured toward his exo-suit. "The armor I wear is barely enough to protect me. I already put you in enough danger as it is. I can't risk your safety more than I already am."

Isabell threw her hands up in frustration. "That's the issue, Ben. I see the difference you make in the world. I see the lives you save. I want to make the same type of difference in the world that you do. I want to save lives. I have a drive in me, an anger, a need to go out there in the world and stop those monsters and slashers."

She placed her hand on Ben's chest. "I also need more from you. I want to be with you, but I can't do that as just your pilot. I need to be your equal, your partner. Just like you feel as if you can't put me in any more danger, I feel the same way. I can't put you in danger without feeling like I'm sharing that responsibility, like we are protecting each other's backs.

"If we can do that, if we can operate as partners out there, I think we can be partners in other ways too." She sighed. "I want to share my life with you, and I want you to share your life with me… I love you. I love you as Ben Watkins and as Raptor, and I want to be with you in each of your identities. I feel that by fully sharing my life with you as both Ben and Raptor that I will feel fulfilled. I'll feel like I am making the difference I need to in the world. I feel like I will be taking the anger pent up in me and channeling it into a positive endeavor."

She wrapped her arms around Ben and hugged him. "I'll also feel that if I am by your side fighting next to you, that you will feel more fulfilled too, that you will be happier. If I'm wrong about that, please let me know. If you don't feel the same way about me that I feel about you, please say so now and I will help you find a replacement for me and then move on with my life."

Ben's answer was to give Isabell a long and passionate kiss.

When he finally pulled away, he looked into her eyes and said, "I do feel that way about you. I am concerned about putting you in more danger, but I can't lose you either. Please help me with this current mission. Help me to stop

Retribution and her revenants and then we can take a serious look about how we can both move forward together."

Isabell kissed him again and replied, "All right. Let me get the plane ready, but I am looking forward to that talk later."

As she walked away Ben took a deep breath. He knew that Isabell was everything he wanted in life. Right now, though, he knew that if they were ever going to have that talk, he would have to survive the mission at the CIA hub and then whatever else Retribution had coming his way.

In order to do that, he needed to be fully focused as Raptor. He took another deep breath and put his helmet back on, thus changing his persona from Ben Watkins back into Raptor.

CHAPTER 16

Both Raptor and Isabell were quiet as the plane flew toward the CIA hub. For the most part, Raptor was mentally preparing himself for what he was about to do. However, he would have been lying to himself if he said that was the only reason, he was quiet. The kiss and brief conversation he had with Isabell was weighing on his mind. He knew he had feelings for her, but until yesterday they almost felt like a schoolboy's daydream. Isabell had always seemed the woman of his dreams who was just out of his reach. She felt out of his reach as well, because of the choices he had made. She was out of reach because he was Raptor.

He lived a dangerous life and he had partially let Isabell into that life, and now she wanted to be even deeper into it. This was what weighed most on his mind. Not only because he already worried about her safety without making her a more active participant in his role as Raptor, but because he wondered if he may have subconsciously set her on this path.

When he first recruited Isabell, he knew he was attracted to her. He knew from her background that she was a person who would be drawn to the life he lived as Raptor. Even with that knowledge, he opened the door to that part of his life for her. Then he asked her to go deeper into it by watching over gangsters… whom he knew could push her to use violence. If he was honest with himself, he knew that once Isabell felt that rush, she would most likely want more.

The question Raptor had to ask himself was did he set her on that path, with the hope that when she went down that road she would want more? And if she wanted more, would she then be in a position to be more than just his pilot?

Raptor knew how intelligent he was, and now he wondered if he had manipulated this amazing woman into changing from the daydream just out of his reach to a woman, he could have a relationship with. Then he wondered if he did all this knowing the potential danger to her health.

He was mired in these thoughts when Isabell's voice came through his visor: "We're coming up on target."

Raptor took a deep breath and pushed his self-reflective thoughts aside. He had a mission to attend to and that is where his focus needed to be. If there was any chance of Isabell having a deeper role in his life, he would need to push his feelings for her aside during a mission.

He opened the door to the plane and felt the intense wind rushing past him. He replied to Isabell, "Stealth mode activated. Preparing to jump in three... two... one."

Raptor then leaped out into the night sky.

The hero felt the wind whipping past him as his speed increased. He counted to ten, then he activated the parachute action of his cape. Raptor's cape opened behind him and slowed his descent.

"Activate night vision!" He shouted into his visor.

Raptor's view changed to the form he had requested. He could see the hub below him, along with a lone car moving down the road that led to and from the motel.

Ahead of the car, just past the motel he saw something else moving which he couldn't identify.

He yelled into his visor, "Show me an electromagnetic view."

His visor switched views again and showed two electromagnetic signatures in the area behind the car. One of the signatures was small but the other was large and increasing in size by the second.

"Activate drone and fly to my position! Eric, Isabell, the parameters of this mission have just changed from an infiltration and interrogation to a rescue. Isabell, I need you to return with the plane to the airport, then get in the helicopter and take it back to the warehouse. When you get there, I need you to set up the scales I took from the statue of Justice. Then place the sword from Grant on one end of it and one of the cords for my grappling hook on the other side."

Isabell's voice came back, "Will your grappling hook cord count as a whip that represents justice?"

"I don't know but we are going to have to hope it does. I'm also going to send you a prayer to Nemesis. I need you to print it up and be prepared to recite it."

"Copy that. I am turning the plane around. I think I can get back to the warehouse in about twenty minutes."

"Eric, get to that motel," Raptor commanded. "I am going to find Agent Desopo. When I do, I will contact you to pull around to the back of the motel. We'll put Desopo into the car and then you need to make it back to the warehouse as soon as possible."

"Copy that, sir," Eric's voice crackled back. "I have pulled the car to the side of the road and turned off the lights. Sir, what about the distraction I was supposed to create?"

Raptor looked at the ever growing second electromagnetic signature. "I don't think a distraction is going to be an issue."

Retribution was floating above the road just past the motel. She was staring at the ground when she suddenly looked down the highway and then up into the sky.

The goddess smiled. "Have the Fates brought all of the people my revenants are looking for to the same location for me?" She waved her hand over the road before her, causing Chester Mansfield's face to appear in it. Retribution then peered down into Mansfield's eyes. "This is different from the liquid rock you have been composed of thus far, but I think for our purposes it will do."

Mansfield's face started to rise as the asphalt of the road itself began to form a large spire. After a few seconds, the revenant's seven-foot-tall body had been remade from the black asphalt of the street.

Retribution looked down the road at the CIA hub. "Perhaps we will give you a bit more to work with this time as well."

She waved her right hand again, causing more of the street to tear itself from the ground and attach to Mansfield's body. As the golem's rocky form continued to grow, she waved her left hand in front of her. This second gesture caused Charles Donnor's body to form in front of her, complete with the potato sack over his head and his fire axe in hand.

The goddess looked at the undead basketball player and pointed down the road toward the hub.

"If you walk down this path," she said, "you shall find the one known as the Barracuda in a vehicle. Fear not that Raptor will alert him to your coming. I have removed the device which Raptor placed in your body and was using to track your whereabouts. It is now discarded in the tunnels where the water drains. He will think you are simply sitting there as you hack the Barracuda to pieces for what he did to you."

Charles grunted in acknowledgement. The six-foot-four ghoul then walked past what was now Chester Mansfield's shin.

Raptor landed on the ground roughly fifty feet from the CIA hub. He started moving toward the motel when he felt the first impact tremor. The hero was in a full sprint when the second tremor shook the ground. CIA agents were pouring out of hotel rooms and into the parking lot as the fifty-foot-tall asphalt golem peered down at the motel.

Agent Desopo was standing in the middle of the parking lot with Silva and Liddel on either side of him. There were roughly thirty other agents in the parking lot as well. They were all staring in awe, at the giant golem who was coming closer to them with each step.

Desopo shook his head in disbelief as he said, "First Raptor, then McConnel is killed by something weird, and now this?"

Liddel pointed to the golem. "What do you want us to do about that thing?"

"Grab the guns from my trunk and waste it!" Desopo shouted.

Agents ran to Desopo's car and grabbed the high-powered rifles he had there. They then turned and fired on the gargantuan golem. Pieces of asphalt flew off the monster as he stalked toward the hub.

Desopo watched in disbelief as the golem continued to move forward through his agents' fusillade. The asphalt colossus took a step into the parking lot and looked directly at Desopo. The creature moaned, lifted its right foot off the ground, and brought it crashing down on five agents, crushing them beneath its massive weight.

Desopo saw the golem looking down at him and he started to walk backwards toward his car. He had only taken a few steps when a pair of powerful hands wrapped around his neck and mouth.

Raptor lifted Desopo off the ground and pulled him around the corner toward the back of the motel. He shouted into his visor, "I have Desopo! Quickly, bring the car around the back of the motel!"

Eric switched on the lights of his car to see the undead form of Charles Donnor standing in front of his vehicle. He quickly threw the vehicle into reverse and backed it up as Charles lifted the axe over his head and brought it

121

crashing into the ground where the hood of Eric's car was only a moment before.

Eric pulled the car onto the road. He was driving toward the motel when Charles' hand smashed through the back window revealing the Barracuda and his men. The sound of the window shattering woke up the mobster and his bodyguards. The gangsters took one look at the revenant and they all began screaming hysterically.

Charles reached into the back seat of the car and grabbed one of the bodyguards as Eric floored the gas pedal and dragged the revenant along with him.

"We're on our way, sir," he replied to Raptor. "I have to inform you that Charles has appeared without warning and he is currently attacking the car."

"Acknowledged," Raptor said with a sigh. "I'll be ready for him when you come around."

The hero was still holding onto Desopo as the kaiju-sized golem brought his fist crashing down on several more agents, instantly ending their lives.

"What happened to Chester Mansfield?" Raptor yelled into the agent's ear so that he could hear him over the gunfire.

Desopo struggled to free himself, "I don't know what you're talking about!"

Retribution appeared in front of Desopo and Raptor. She shook her head at the agent as she said, "You're lying. After Ben Watkins turned down the offer you had him orchestrate, you sent Mansfield to break into Watkins' office with Silva and Liddel to steal prototypes to sell to those men in the warehouse. Then after Raptor chased Mansfield off, you and McConnel buried him in concrete."

"Mansfield cried out for revenge and I brought him back." She pointed to the huge golem as it crushed three more men beneath his huge asphalt foot. "That is him now!"

Desopo looked up at the giant as his men continued to fire in vain at the massive creature.

Retribution then continued to explain to Desopo what she had done. "He already killed Agent McConnel and the men that you were going to sell the guns to. Those men died because they tried to stop Mansfield from getting his revenge."

The monster seemed to let out a deep and anguished moan as it bent down through the hail of gunfire, grabbed two men, and lifted them over his head.

The golem slowly squeezed the two until their bodies were crushed from the pressure.

"That was agents Silva and Liddel," the goddess said to Raptor and Desopo with a smile. "I guess that just leaves you two for Mansfield to gain revenge on."

Raptor saw the car turning into the parking lot with Charles hanging onto the side of the window and reaching for the Barracuda. He watched as the revenant closed his hand on one of the bodyguard's face and crushed. The monster then pulled the man's body out of the vehicle by what was left of his head and tossed it to the ground while holding onto the still moving car.

"Call your men off and tell them to run!" Raptor yelled to Desopo. "Mansfield is only after us! He won't kill your agents if they are not protecting you!"

He tossed Desopo aside and turned his attention toward the oncoming car.

The CIA agent took one look at the golem that was Chester Mansfield and yelled, "Keep firing! That thing will eventually fall!"

He then made a break for his car. Raptor cursed when he heard what Desopo had commanded.

The car with Charles still hanging on the side of it had nearly reached him and the hero knew that he had only one chance to dislodge the monster and save the Barracuda. The vehicle was speeding toward Raptor at over sixty miles per hour. It was roughly thirty feet away from the vigilante when he leaped into the air and extended his leg.

Raptor timed his flying kick perfectly. His foot connected with Charles' jaw. The force of the impact forced the revenant to relinquish his hold on the car and sent him tumbling across the ground. Raptor himself fell to the ground with his leg aching. Even with his exo-suit absorbing most of the impact, hitting a target moving at such a high speed had taken a toll on his body. Raptor ignored the throbbing pain and forced himself to stand up and continue the battle.

As Charles was beginning to stand Raptor threw one of the spheres from his bandoliers at the zombie. The rounded device exploded next to Charles and covered him in liquid nitrogen.

"We have been through this, hero," Retribution said with an exasperated sigh. "You know that won't stop him."

Raptor ignored the goddess, spun around, and fired one of the batons from his gauntlet at Desopo. The baton struck the agent in the back and sent an electric shock running through his body as he was climbing into his car. Desopo fell to the ground shaking from the jolt he had received as Eric pulled the limo up next to him.

After Raptor had sprinted over to Desopo, he looked up to see Mansfield bring his foot down on four more CIA agents, crushing them like insects, while their fellow agents continued to fire upon the golem.

Raptor grabbed the still shaking form of Desopo, opened the door to the limo, and threw him in the back of the car with the Barracuda and his remaining bodyguard. From the smell that permeated the vehicle, the vigilante could tell that either the Barracuda or the bodyguard had voided his bowels as Charles was reaching for them.

Raptor slammed the door shut and yelled into his visor, "Eric, get back to the warehouse now!"

Eric spun the car around, turned on the nitrous boosters his family had added to the vehicle's components, and sped out of the parking lot.

Raptor turned around to see Retribution floating in the air next to Charles and waving her hand over him. As she did this the revenant started breaking free of the ice, he was encased in. The crime fighter quickly looked behind him to see that of the thirty agents who had first engaged the golem only half of them were left alive and they were still trying to stop Mansfield based on Desopo's last order.

Raptor was trapped between the zombified Charles Donnor and the colossal golem that was Charles Mansfield. An alert flashed across his visor, indicating that his drone was overhead.

Raptor gritted his teeth and said, "Activate voice amplifier and exo-suit drone magnetic connection."

The hero looked to the sky to see his drone streaking down toward him. When it was above his head he leaped into the air. When he hit the apex of his leap the drone's magnetic field grabbed a hold of the crime fighter and pulled him to it. Raptor felt a thud as his back attached to the bottom of the drone, effectively turning it into a jetpack.

He used the controls in his gauntlets to switch the drone over to manual control and then flew over the agents who were still trying to stop the golem. He turned the amplifier to its maximum setting so they could hear him over the gunfire and the noise Mansfield was making.

"Attention CIA agents! Disperse! Desopo is gone and the monster will not chase you if you flee!"

Raptor looped over the motel one more time and sailed toward the golem. He was glad to see that most of the agents had listened to him as they were running away from the motel.

The soaring vigilante armed the drone's missiles and fired them at Mansfield. The missiles exploded on the golem' chest and caused its asphalt body to fall to the ground in pieces. The hero circled over the rubble and he saw the seven-foot concrete form of Mansfield climbing out of the pile of asphalt that had been its larger body.

Raptor then flew over to where Charles Donnor was standing with Retribution floating in the air next to him. He looked at the goddess as he called out a challenge.

"I have the Barracuda and Desopo! All three of us will be at my base of operations! I assume you know where that is! Meet us there! One way or another this ends tonight!"

He then flew off in the direction of his lair.

The concrete-encased Mansfield walked over next to where Retribution and Charles were standing. The goddess looked at her revenants as a devious smile formed on her face as she spoke to them.

"All right, boys! It looks like we are all going to get what we want tonight."

CHAPTER 17

Isabell brought the helicopter down in the warehouse parking lot. She ran inside and grabbed the scales Raptor had taken from the statue of Lady Justice as well as Ulysses S. Grant's sword. She then grabbed a flashlight and cursed out Raptor for always keeping his lair dark.

The pilot made her way down the dark stairway and into Raptor's lair as quickly as she could. She ran over to the wall where Raptor kept his reserve weapons, grabbed one of the rods for his gauntlets with a rope in it, and then ran back up the stairs.

As Isabell made her way back upstairs, she heard Raptor's drone circling overhead. She placed the rod/rope with the other artifacts and then sprinted over to her computer console and printed up the prayer Raptor had sent her to summon Nemesis.

Isabell grabbed the paper off the printer as Raptor walked into the building. It was clear from the way he was limping that the hero was hurt.

She ran over to the crime fighter and wrapped her arms around him. "Are you okay?"

He nodded and replied, "I'll be fine; maybe some internal bruising, but nothing I can't fight through."

Isabell pointed to the scales, sword, and rope. "I got all the stuff you requested, ready to go. Should we start the summoning now?"

Before Raptor could answer, they heard Eric's car peel into the parking lot. The driver pulled the car into the warehouse through the bay doors. He then stepped out and opened the passenger door to show Desopo, the Barracuda, and the remaining bodyguard.

Desopo crawled out of the car and went to run for the large bay doors when the concrete in front of the entrances began to shake and crack. The CIA agent took several steps back as the concrete ripped itself off the ground and formed a huge seven-foot-tall pillar. The column began to shift and change shape as arms, legs, and a head all branched out from the concrete body. When the golem was fully formed it fixed its blank stare on Desopo.

A loud splashing sound could be heard coming from the river outside of the warehouse. The people gathered inside the building looked out the bay doors to see the pale, gray skinned, hulking form of Charles Donnor climbing out of the river with his axe in hand. As the revenant walked toward the bay doors, he adjusted the sack over his head so that his eyes could see through the slits the Barracuda had cut out for him. Charles walked over next to the Mansfield golem and stood next to him.

The two giants were staring at the gathered people as Raptor whispered to Isabell, "Take the artifacts to the back of the warehouse and recite the incantation. See if you can summon Nemesis. I'll try to buy you as much time as I can."

Isabell grabbed the artifacts and ran to the back of the building.

Raptor looked back toward the revenant and the golem to see Retribution floating between them.

The vengeance goddess smiled as she looked at the people gathered before her. She then fixed her gaze on Raptor.

"You have not only trapped yourself," she said, "but you have also gathered the others I am hunting together for me and trapped them as well. Did you realize that your efforts are in vain and have decided to submit to punishment? Or, is this some last-ditch effort to make a final stand?"

Raptor raised his fists in front of him as he looked at the Barracuda and Desopo. "Get behind me!"

He then charged at the two monsters. Raptor delivered a stiff jab to Charles' face that would have shattered a normal man's jaw. Despite having enough force to shatter a cinderblock, the blow only managed to cause the undead athlete to slightly turn his head.

The revenant swung his axe at Raptor, but the vigilante dodged the blow and then hit Mansfield's knee with a thrust kick that displaced the golem's foot and caused him to fall on his face. The hero then looked back at Charles to see the monster's axe coming down at him. Raptor side-stepped the attack and let the axe strike the concrete-covered shoulder of Chester Mansfield.

Charles had swung the axe with such force that it buried itself in the golem's stony hide. As the undead athlete was trying to pull his axe free from the golem, Raptor hit the zombie with two hooks to the ribs, an uppercut to the face, and a knee to the solar plexus. The exo-suit enhanced blows had no effect on the revenant, unfortunately, and with one swing of his hand, he struck the crime fighter in the ribs and sent him sprawling to the floor.

Raptor rolled with the blow as best as he could. He then stood to see Mansfield looming over him and Charles making his way toward the Barracuda with his axe lifted over his head.

The golem reached out for Raptor, but the crime fighter ducked under the grab attempt and then ran past the stone giant. Charles had almost reached the Barracuda – who was paralyzed with fear – when the vigilante dove at the giant's feet and wrapped his arms around the monster's knees. The undead brute fell hard on the floor, landing face first. There was a sickening splat when the revenant's face hit the floor, which caused salt water and seaweed to expel from his mouth.

Raptor was in the middle of standing up when Mansfield grabbed him by the back of the neck and lifted him into the air. The golem struck the hero in the chest with enough force to crack his ribs through the protective exo-suit.

Raptor looked to his left to see Retribution floating there. The goddess smiled as she looked at Raptor like a hungry predator.

"This is it, hero," she said. "This is where you die for your part in Chester Mansfield's death."

As Raptor was battling the two revenants, Isabell placed Grant's sword and Raptor's baton on the scales. She then pulled out the print up of the incantation to summon Nemesis. She then began the recitation.

"I praise bright-eyed Nemesis, daughter of dark-cloaked Nyx. Nemesis who watches, who knows whenever we have done harm, who makes certain that all evil is punished, that all who are guilty receive their due;

"Swift-winged Nemesis, bearer of the apple branch, in days of old were you well honored, goddess, by those who suffered the losses and pains of love;

"Many were the false-hearted lovers who felt your wrath. Fair-minded Nemesis, just one, unyielding one, you are the firmest foe of cruel and violent men;

"You are the avenger of the wronged, the disperser of right reward. Nemesis, I honor you."

The interior of the warehouse was suddenly lit by a burst of flames that filled the entire structure of the building. Isabell instinctively shielded her eyes when she saw the flames coming toward her. Her body shook when the fire reached her, but she was both surprised and relieved when the flames did not burn her.

Isabell looked around the room to see the flames imploding in on itself and collapsing into a single point in front of her. The flames molded themselves into a humanoid shape with wings.

"An angel," Isabell whispered to herself.

The flames began to fall away from the humanoid form to reveal a winged woman who was both beautiful and terrifying at the same time.

As she looked at the woman floating before her Isabell whispered a line, she recalled from the movie *Hellraiser*: "Angels to some, demons to others."

The goddess Nemesis looked around the room. When Mansfield saw her, the golem immediately dropped Raptor and fell to one knee. Charles Donnor placed his axe on the floor and kneeled as well.

Even Retribution floated over toward Nemesis and fell to a knee before the divine goddess. She then bowed her head and simply said, "Mistress."

With the two revenants, Retribution, and Raptor were all on the ground, the Barracuda, his bodyguard, and Desopo all fled the warehouse.

Nemesis looked down at her servant and spoke in voice that had the hollow tone of Retribution's voice but with a far grimmer tone to it.

"Retribution, why have I been summoned?"

Retribution shook her head and replied, "It was not I who summoned you, oh mighty Nemesis. It was the mortal female."

Nemesis' eyes were literally burning with anger as she turned her head toward Isabell. *"Mortal, by what right do you see fit to call upon the Goddess of Vengeance?"*

Raptor removed his helmet as he intrepidly limped over toward Nemesis,

"She called you on my behalf," the vigilante said as he walked up to Nemesis. "I needed to summon you because it is my understanding that you are

129

the goddess of not only vengeance but also of judicial punishment. Is that statement true?

Nemesis looked down at Raptor and replied, *"These words are indeed true. Now state why you have called me. I have matters to attend to far beyond the scope of mortal understanding."* She pointed to Retribution. *"This is why I have appointed my servant to act in my stead in mortal affairs."*

Raptor knelt down in front of Nemesis. "Then it is with utmost respect for you that I would suggest your servant is not fulfilling her role as you intended. She is dispensing vengeance on humans, but she is doing so without any concern for judicial punishment."

Nemesis turned her gaze upon Retribution. *"Servant, is this true?"*

Retribution glared at Raptor in anger and then she looked back at Nemesis as she gestured to her revenants. "The men behind me were murdered! They cried out for vengeance against those who murdered them! Is it not judicial punishment that they slay those whom they hold accountable for having their very lives taken from them?"

Nemesis turned and addressed Raptor. *"Caped one, what do you say in response to this claim?"*

"Those men were murdered," he said, "and those that killed them will be brought to justice. This I swear to you. But even beyond killing those directly responsible for the murder of the creatures standing behind me, Retribution has understated the extent to which she has let her creations go on a killing spree.

"There was one man whom after he murdered the person who killed him, turned and tried to kill those who watched him die. I knew this man. In life, he was a criminal who served time for his crimes and then he tried to make amends with what remained of his life by helping me stop crime in the city. When I appealed to his better nature with this argument, he rejected the vengeance he was seeking."

Nemesis turned her attention to Retribution who quickly tried to justify her actions. "The man in question was also killed with two beasts. I brought the three of them back as one revenant to seek revenge. Even if the man decided he did not desire revenge, the beasts still did."

"The people who were spectators will face justice," Raptor quickly interjected. "They will pay for their crimes and then be given the chance to still make a positive difference in this world. Wouldn't that be a more judicial punishment than death?"

"What if you were those beasts?" Retribution screamed at Raptor. "What if you had watched those men cheer as you were murdered? Wouldn't you want those men to die?"

Raptor shook his head. "Judicial punishment cannot not be carried out through the scope of one individual's biased view. Judicial punishment can only be handed out through the objective perspective of an unbiased third party."

Retribution looked at Nemesis when responding to that. "Mistress, long ago did you not appoint me to be that third party? To assess who was guilty and then to enact vengeance on those who deserve it?"

Before Nemesis could answer, Raptor spoke up. "Your own words prove you have gone beyond the scope of the task assigned to you!" He pointed to the golem that was once Chester Mansfield. "That man there was murdered by one of the men who fled this room and several others. He held them responsible for his death. He also held *me* responsible for his death because as Ben Watkins I refused to allow him to use my resources to create weapons that would kill innocent people.

"Then, as Raptor, I stopped him from taking those same resources from my building. I had no intention of killing Chester for these actions. Subjecting him to the consequences of the law to face prison time, yes; but I never intended to kill him."

Raptor stood up and took a step closer to Nemesis before continuing his spiel. "I ask you, oh goddess of judicial punishment and vengeance, would an objective third party deem my actions worthy of death? Or has Retribution's bloodlust reached a point where she will give anyone who holds another responsible for their death, regardless of their actions, the means to kill that person simply to satisfy her own need for killing?"

Nemesis raised her hand. *"I have heard enough!"*

The winged goddess then looked at Retribution.

"Long ago, when you were still human, you summoned me with a sword and whip used for dispensing justice. As a human who sought to fight against the evils committed by man, I deemed you capable of determining how to balance revenge and judicial punishment."

Nemesis then turned to Raptor. *"This human believes that either you have lost your way, or that how humans perceive the distinction between judicial punishment and vengeance has changed over the millennia. As the goddess of judicial punishment and vengeance it is my task to enforce these concepts*

131

across the cosmos. It is up to each manner of being within the cosmos to determine how their society sees fit to define these concepts."

She looked toward Retribution. *"Do you still have the sword you brought before me?"*

"Of course, Mistress," Retribution said as she unsheathed her sword.

Nemesis nodded. *"Then as the scales of justice are balanced by the objects which battle for supremacy on either side of it, so am I. Another human who has fought against the evils of man may take hold of a sword of justice and challenge Retribution for her role as my avatar."*

Raptor took a step toward Grant's sword when Isabell suddenly lifted the blade above her head. "I will challenge her for the role as your avatar!"

"Isabell, no!" Raptor screamed.

Nemesis ignored the hero's objection and granted Isabell the power to challenge Retribution.

Grant's sword burst into flames and Isabell found herself in the same tight fitting leather outfit and overcoat that Retribution wore.

Retribution screamed and charged at Isabell with her own flaming sword in hand. The blonde-haired goddess' attack on Isabell was furious. The former Air Force pilot had trained with large knives during her time in the military, but she had never really handled a sword before. By contrast, Retribution had been a human in the time when people lived and died by the sword. She was well versed in the art of using a blade to kill people.

Isabell was barely managing to block Retribution's attacks when the blonde goddess suddenly rose into the air and swung her blade down at the pilot from above.

She partially blocked the attack but as Retribution's sword slid off the pilot's blade it sliced across her shoulder.

Realizing she now had the powers of a god as well; Isabell leaped into the air and was now floating above the floor. She screamed and swung her sword at Retribution. The blonde blocked Isabell's attack and then flew below her.

Retribution came up behind Isabell and thrust her sword at her. Once more the pilot was only able to partially deflect the attack. Isabell blocked the sword from impaling her but deflected it in such a manner that it grazed her side, giving her a second wound.

Raptor watched as the woman he loved fought for both their lives. He yelled out, "Isabell, don't fight her fight! Fight *yours!* You're not a fencer! You're a kickboxer!"

Isabell's eyes went wide when she heard what Raptor had said. When Retribution attempted her next thrust, the pilot ducked under the attack, moved closer to Retribution and punched her in the face. The blow stunned Retribution. Isabell then kicked her opponent's sword hand causing her to drop her weapon.

Isabell threw her sword to the ground. She then pummeled Retribution with a series of kicks and punches. Retribution's face was a bloody mess when Isabell delivered a thrust kick to her chin that sent the blonde crashing back to the floor of the warehouse.

Retribution looked up from the ground at Isabell and said, "Go ahead, extract your vengeance for me threatening the life of your lover. Kill me and take my place."

Isabell shook her head and responded in the same ghostly voice as Retribution. "No. I understand the difference between judicial punishment and vengeance. I will not take a life when none has been taken. Your punishment will be to live as a human in the world you have lost contact with. Hopefully, as you pay for your crime you will learn to make amends for the wrongs you have done."

She then waved her hand over Retribution, which caused a ball of fire to swarm around her body. Isabell raised her hand, lifted the flames off Retribution's body, and absorbed them into herself.

The now human Retribution looked at Isabell and decreed "You cannot do this. You should have killed me. You should have killed me!"

Isabell shook her head. "I have rendered my decision. Now go and learn the difference between justice and vengeance." With a second wave of Isabell's hand, Retribution disappeared.

Isabell then turned to Charles Donnor and Chester Mansfield. "You have been turned into monsters. You have committed acts as deplorable or worse than those committed against you. Go now and rest. Those who have wronged you will be brought to justice."

She waved her hand at the two revenants and as it passed over them, they turned to dust.

Isabell next addressed Nemesis. "Thank you for the power you have given me. From now on I will act in your stead on this planet." She looked over her body. "I can feel the rage of those who unjustly died calling out for vengeance. Their calls are strong. I can understand why Retribution acted in the manner she did."

Isabell turned her head and looked at Raptor. "Unlike your previous avatar, I shall not let those who have died decide who deserves punishment. I shall bring those who commit wrong to justice." She smiled at the man she loved. "I have an example to look to who will help me distinguish the fine line between justice and vengeance." Turning back to Nemesis, she said, "I have but one request. I do not wish to be known as Retribution. I should prefer to be called Divine Justice."

Nemesis nodded her approval. *"So be it! Go forth, Divine Justice, and deal with those who have harmed others as is in accordance with justice, in my name."*

There was a bright flash of light and then Nemesis was gone.

Raptor walked over toward Divine Justice. "Isabell," he said solemnly. "I... I don't know what to say. You... you're a goddess now."

She grabbed Raptor, pulled him toward her, and kissed him.

"I can't explain it all to you now. The powers flowing through me are beyond my ability to verbalize." She looked him in the eye. "What I can tell you is that I now know we can have what we wanted. We can fight evil side by side. I can be with you without you worrying about me being harmed. I can right wrongs and fight evil on a worldwide scale now."

She kissed him again. "I also know this means I can be with you. You and I can have a life together. I just need some time to grow accustomed to my new powers. I love you and we *will* be together, but right now I need to leave. When I understand what I have become I will be back for you."

There was a flash of light and she was gone.

Raptor was standing in the middle of the warehouse looking down at the floor with tears in his eyes.

Eric picked up Raptor's helmet and brought it over to him. He handed the head covering to his friend.

"Sir, I could see it in her eyes. Even after her transformation, Isabell loves you more than anything else in the world. I have no doubt that she will be true to her word. She will be back. Additionally, she is what she is now because of you. Because of what you taught her and the opportunities you gave her. Most importantly, though – and I know you could see this as well as I – because of you, she is happy."

Raptor took his helmet from his friend and wiped his eyes. "I know she'll be back. When she returns, let's make sure she is proud of us. We need to get to work on tracking down the Barracuda and Desopo and bringing them to justice."

Eric grabbed his boss' shoulder. "Just one question, sir. Are you going to require me to take pilot lessons?"

Raptor laughed and replied, "Let me return the scales of justice to their rightful place and see how much it's going to cost to get a replica of Grant's sword made first. Then, we'll see about flying lessons."

EPILOGUE

It had taken Raptor three months since he had lost him in the warehouse, but the vigilante had finally tracked down Agent Desopo. The intelligence operative was now stationed in a CIA hub outside of Chicago.

The building itself was a former five story hotel, and his best guess was that Desopo was in the middle of it. Raptor was perched on the ledge of a building across the street from the hotel. He was hidden in shadows with his suit in stealth mode as his drone was flying around the hotel and performing a thermal scan of the building to determine how many agents he was going to have to fight through or elude to bring Desopo to justice.

The drone was halfway through its scan when a bright light appeared behind Raptor and a hollow voice whispered in his ear. "There are thirty men in the building, counting Desopo. Well, eighteen men and twelve women to be exact."

Raptor spun around to see Isabell standing there garbed in a dark, red leather halter top and mini-skirt, along with a long coat and Grant's flaming sword in her hand. She grabbed Raptor by the shoulder, leaned in close to him, phased her face through his visor, and kissed him.

When she pulled away, Raptor shook his head in disbelief. "Isabell, you can kiss me through my visor?"

"That's not all I can do." She held her hand out in front of her, directed it at the hotel, and then clenched it into a fist. As she closed her hand the lights in the hotel turned off. Raptor switched his helmet over to night vision to see that the CIA agents were now scrambling throughout the building.

He shook his head. "Isabell, is there any limit to what you can do?"

"I can't seem to change this outfit. I guess it is sort of my uniform now. I can change the color so I'm not all in black like my predecessor." She pressed her body against Raptor's. "I can also take it off. Otherwise, while I've learned a lot about my abilities over the past three months, I'm still not sure of their full extent. I was hoping we could find out together."

Raptor took half step away from her. "Nothing would make me happier, but first let's bring Desopo to justice. Then we'll take down the Barracuda."

She nodded. "All right, but after that you and I are going to enjoy ourselves for a little bit. Even if I have to freeze time to do it."

Raptor shook his head a third time. "Can you actually do that?"

Her only reply was a coy smile.

Raptor had never seen Isabell so happy and that made him happy as well. Given the power Isabell had displayed, she also clearly was no longer going to be in any danger if she accompanied him on his missions. For the first time, he truly felt that they could be happy together.

She laughed. "And all it took was me to become a goddess for that to happen for us."

Raptor had a startled look on his face. "Were you just reading my mind?"

She gave a coy smile again. "As far as I know, I don't have the ability to read minds, but I can see your face through your visor. From the look on it, I could tell exactly what you were thinking."

He shrugged. "We need to take advantage of the blackout, and grab Desopo while the agents are still confused by it." He looked at her flaming sword. "Isabell, are you able to turn off the bright flames on that sword of yours?"

She lifted the sword above her head and the flames changed from bright orange to pitch black. "Yes, I can. And when we are in the field, Raptor, please call me Divine Justice."

Raptor nodded in reply and the two heroes leapt off the building and into the night.

END

ABOUT THE AUTHOR

Matt Dennion lives in New Jersey with his wife, two daughters, and their two dogs. Matt works primarily as a teacher of Students with Autism and as a Work-Based Learning Coordinator. He has loved giant monster and superhero stories his entire life. He began writing short stories for Black Coat Press and *G-Fan* magazine in 2007.

In 2015 he began writing kaiju novels for Severed Press. His current works for Severed Press include *Chimera: Scourge of the Gods*; *Operation: ROC*; *Atomic Rex*; *Polar Yeti and the Beasts of Prehistory*; *Atomic Rex: Wrath of the Polar Yeti*; *Kaiju Corps*; *Atomic Rex: Conquest of Chimera*; *Operation Megalodon*; *Valley of the Dinosaurs*; *Marsh Thing*; and the soon to be released *Atomic Rex: Challenge of Gurral*.

He has also written comic books in collaboration with other creators. His comic works include *Draco Azul/ Atomic Rex: Shadow of the Raptor* with Andres Perez; *Atomic Rex vs. Dorugan* with Chris Martinez; *and Irokus x Atomic Rex: Avatars of the Apocalypse* Parts 1 and 2 with Frank Parr and Wayne Smith.

Matthew has a line of superhero novels including *The Kaiju and the Crime Fighter and Other Kaiju Tales* (self-published); *Raptor Tales: Heroes and Monsters* for Kaiju vs. Cancer; and *Raptor: Revenge of the Revenants* for Wild Hunt Press. He has also self-published the kaiju anthology *Kaiju Tales* and the illustrated children's book *Frankenstein's Monster Goes to OZ*.

All of Matt's novels, anthologies, and comics are available on Amazon in print and digital formats. Along with his friends Andres Perez and Chris Martinez, Matt has also created the charity Kaiju vs Cancer, through which creators use their monsters and heroes to team with St. Jude Children Research Hospital to battle childhood cancer! Multi-author anthologies published under that charity label have included the aforementioned *Raptor Tales: Heroes and Monsters* and *Courage on Infinite Earths.*

Contact info:

mjd5538@yahoo.com

Links:

Google Sites - https://sites.google.com/view/matthew-dennion-author-page/home

Amazon Author Page - https://www.amazon.com/Matthew-Dennion/e/B01I2CYODQ

Facebook - https://www.facebook.com/Matthew-Dennion-457021674465039

Twitter - @PASCMatt1

Kaiju vs. Cancer Facebook Page - https://www.facebook.com/KaijuVsCancer/